THE LOST TRAVELLER

thou art still
The Son of Morn in weary Night's decline,
The Lost Traveller's Dream under the Hill.

WILLIAM BLAKE, "*The Gates of Paradise.*"

The
Lost Traveller

by

Ruthven Todd

With Drawings by John Craxton

DOVER PUBLICATIONS, INC.
NEW YORK

Published in Canada by General Publishing Company, Ltd., 30 Lesmill Road, Don Mills, Toronto, Ontario.
Published in the United Kingdom by Constable and Company, Ltd., 10 Orange Street, London WC 2.

This Dover edition, first published in 1968, is an unabridged and unaltered republication of the work originally published by the Grey Walls Press in London in 1943. A new Preface has been written by the author for this edition.

International Standard Book Number: 0-486-22191-1
Library of Congress Catalog Card Number: 68-29041

Manufactured in the United States of America
Dover Publications, Inc.
180 Varick Street
New York, N. Y. 10014

TO NICOLETTE BERNARD

Somehow the tired reach home,
The lost pigeons find their cote ;
So the heart shelters underneath a name,
The horror of the dream becomes remote

AN ATTEMPT AT A PREFACE

HOW did my imagination work some thirty years ago? And why did it produce the things it did? I have suddenly been faced with these questions by a paragraph in a letter from Mr. Hayward Cirker, president of Dover Publications, who writes: "We like *The Lost Traveller,* but our editors think that a postscript or a new introduction telling how you came to write the book, or an indication of its symbolic meaning, would be helpful."

I find this a difficult note to answer, and I can only approach it, peering round now overgrown hedgerows, by trying to do a little bird watching into a barely remembered past.

The Lost Traveller was published by the Grey Walls Press in 1943, after Charles Wrey Gardiner had been assured about it by Alex Comfort, Nicholas Moore and, I think, Fred Marnau.

But its history goes a long way further back than that. So far as I can now recall I wrote a longish first draft of it in 1935 and 1936. This was before, in 1938, under a suddenly renewed influence of Kafka and a good many others, I came to write the novel actually published earliest, *Over the Mountain.*

Over the Mountain was conceived and written before I had read Rex Warner's *The Wild Goose Chase,* and I was, I think, a little chagrined to realize that they were both scions of the same ancestry, and that they both bore some evidence of the political atmosphere of the period of their adolescence. Looking back at them both today, I can see how very different they are both in intent and in achieve-

1

ment. Obviously I had less political purpose, although I was one of the inert minnows in the political stream of that day. Mostly, though, I would say I was merely writing out of the madness which I then enjoyed, while at the same time I was making some effort to communicate, to make my peculiarities acceptable to others.

I can recall the writing of *Over the Mountain* almost as clearly today as when I wrote it. I had recently been married and we were visiting my wife's parents in Edinburgh. In Waterston's, a large legal stationery store in George Street, I bought a blue, leather-spined, quarto notebook with narrow ruling. I retired, each morning, to my father-in-law's study. There, surrounded by books on sex and on genetics, for he was F.A.E. Crew, the geneticist and future propagator of Social (having little to do with "Socialist") Medicine, I managed to keep my attention firmly on the job in hand, avoiding the temptations of Malinowski and Krafft-Ebing, the fascinating mutations of the *Drosophila,* and even the genetics of the budgerigar.

For ten or more hours a day, I wrote, in a small and probably rather illegible hand, while making the most intricate doodle on the last flyleaf of the book. Each evening, lying in bed, I would read what I had written to Cicely and she asked for more, despite the fact that there were few cliffhangers. The writing of the manuscript took about eight days and, encouraged by my private and personal audience, I spent about the same number of weeks in typing and revising the book. Then I sought for a publisher.

It seemed doubtful whether, in those uncertain days of 1938 and 1939, I would find anyone willing to publish it. Fortune, however, decreed that a most peculiarly round peg happened at that moment to be sitting in an outstandingly square hole. Geoffrey Grigson was editor at Harrap's. Now Harrap's are an old-established firm, devoted to education and respectability but hardly given to adventure.

2

Geoffrey, struggling against I know not what odds, was doing his best to make them realize that something had happened in the world since the Edwardians had taken a nudge at the Victorians. It was, of course, a vain effort, but, besides managing to get *Over the Mountain* published, I recall, among many other things, that he was the first editor to recognize the promise of Patrick White. (Here, it must be understood, I am writing only about his career at Harrap's, since in all his other incarnations, Geoffrey Grigson has been one of the greatest editors and encouragers of my time.)

Then, I do not know how, Raymond Postgate managed to persuade Blanche Knopf to accept the book for American publication. Mrs. Knopf was visiting England, in search of authors, and was staying in a service flat in Jermyn Street. My memory may be wrong, but I have the impression that she had a dictaphone in every room, including the bathroom. One thing of which I am certain is that when she asked me what I would drink and when I suggested whisky, she countered firmly with a bottle of white wine, a good one.

All this time I was cherishing the drafts of *The Lost Traveller*. These were untidy scraps of paper, not at all like the neat notebook which I later gave Peter Watson as a small mark of gratitude to him for his kindness when I worked on *Horizon* during its early days. I typed out the book at last, but Geoffrey Grigson was gone from Harrap's, and Knopf had not been encouraged by the minuscule sale of *Over the Mountain*. The days of the surrealists were over, when Dent would publish a book such as Hugh Sykes Davis's *Petron*. So the typescript stayed with me and I tinkered with it at intervals, going so far as to type it out once again, and even having it bound.

It was a book which perhaps I had worked out in my unconscious. Early in the Thirties I had become involved with surrealism, but I had found out that I was the owner

3

of too formal a mind to accept the completely illogical or, at times, formless. My "quest," as both novels were concerned with the matter, demanded a certain shape.

Dreams, in spite of this, were for me often as logical as anything in life, and I think that, in all truth, I tended only too often to regard life as if it were an illogical dream. The symbols which people seemed to accept as realities were basically no more concrete than those I found in dreams. The multicolored seeds in a package of bird food were as actual an exchange as any coinage from a bank.

The strange shapes of the personages in a painting by Miró were as real to me as the people on the Underground during the rush hour, whose faces became blanker and less meaningful. The eccentricities of the early Dali paintings were completely credible, and every street down which I walked suffered the loneliness of a painting by de Chirico.

What I think *now* is that I was trying to justify this attitude. In *Over the Mountain* I had tried, a long way after Kafka, to write a quest novel which was valid for my time. In *The Lost Traveller*, the earlier work which I kept by me and which I could not leave alone, I had a book which was to enjoy only its own validities.

I have a strong suspicion that the book came to me not in one dream alone, but rather in a series of dreams, spread over a considerable number of months. The impact of these dreams remained with me, and gradually the pieces began to fit together until they made what seemed *to me* to be a whole, formal in its own shape.

Of course, the things I read played their parts in my dreams. I recognize now, among other things, that the egg-smooth faces come from a Japanese fairy tale retold by Lafcadio Hearn, that Omar probably owes quite a lot to the Bailiff in Wyndham Lewis's *The Childermass*, and that the inescapable end could not have been written without my memory of the story of the last of the Great Auks, beaten to death as a witch by two ignorant fishermen. It is

4

probable that I may even have been aware of these literary echoes when I had first written the book, but they were as much a part of the fabric of my dreams as the paintings to which I have referred. As such, they were equally permissible as material for me, although today I think the book more influenced by painting than by literature.

The Lost Traveller seems to me to be full of symbols which were realities to the young man who tried to weave them into his tapestry. Had I then known "The Unicorn in the Garden" in The Cloisters, New York, I feel sure that Garden would have appeared somewhere, for it has filled my dreams ever since I first saw it. At that time I was only aware of Bosch's visions of Heaven and Hell and, as in almost all paintings, Hell is more vivid and more filled with incident than Paradise. Also, when one is young and knows too little of it, Hell has a fascination beyond that of Heaven, upon the verges of which one always seems to be just about to encroach.

There is no tragedy implicit in the inevitability of this book which was written by a me who no longer exists. If I were to try to rewrite it now, or even to correct it, something would vanish. I wrote it in a kind of vision, a vision in which things took on their own immediate meanings, wherein I had not time to stop and check. I even made the mistake of thinking that a "maroon" was a kind of klaxon, and I must let that remain, for should I start with one wrong word, I would find my pen escape in alteration.

The book was rather longer when Charles Wrey Gardiner decided to publish it, but in 1943 there was a paper shortage in England and he, Alex Comfort, Nicholas Moore and I spent several miserable evenings chopping out pieces so that Gardiner could squeeze out an edition of a thousand copies on his paper quota. Although the printer had not enough paper available to publish the book as it originally stood, a sudden windfall allowed him to print a second edition of another thousand copies. This was a fortuitous happening which meant that I earned a little more from the book than I had expected to do. The deleted pages, however, have never been found.

Today I cannot say anything about the reality of the book. To me it is like one of the sea-washed fragments of glass which I treasured as a child and in which I still find a certain satisfaction. They exist only as themselves and no two pieces are exactly the same, or can appear identical to different finders.

In those days I was most definitely a split personality. There was the me who wrote poems, the me to whom this book belongs, and there was also the me who hankered after being a scholar. While the book remained with me, and while I was nagging at it, I was also editing Alexander Gilchrist's *Life of William Blake,* with a plethora of notes and corrections, for the Everyman's Library, and writing the series of essays which became *Tracks in the Snow* (to be republished, with an added essay, by Dover Publications).

I was simple-minded and I did not realize that my two worlds could not be seen as one by everybody. When I sent Geoffrey Keynes, my good friend and helper in my amateur scholarship, one of the first copies of *The Lost Traveller,* I received by return an explosive letter, failing to understand how anyone, in those days of shortage, could waste valuable paper by printing such utter balderdash. I still remember the hurt that came in recognizing that something which I had created seemed less valuable than my annotations upon the words of others.

RUTHVEN TODD

Galilea, Mallorca
1968

THE LOST TRAVELLER

CHAPTER ONE

T HE country where Christopher found himself was certainly very strange. He had been walking down the street, gazing into the shop windows, when suddenly there had been a loud explosion, the bursting of a gas-main, perhaps, or the result of some act of sabotage and he had been thrown over on his back among the blocks of stone.

The sky had seemed to be blood flowing from a great open wound, and there had been a cry like that of some unearthly beast. The nearest approach to that cry Christopher had ever heard had been one day, a child on holiday in the country, when he had heard squealing from a hut and, expecting a murderer and his victim, had found two men trying to bore a hole in a pig's nose, to fit it with a copper ring.

He had shut his eyes against the brutal sky and would have shut his ears against the screaming, but he could not move. As he fainted, he remembered that the note of a violin, if high enough pitched, could break a wine-glass, and had wondered whether this sound would smash his taut ear-drums, to let his brains flow out through the whorled trumpets.

Now the street had vanished and he was lying among the ruins of a city. Broken columns, delicately fluted, lay in the sand, or stood up towards a clean blue sky, flat as a glazed bowl.

This sudden change in his surroundings made it difficult for him to focus his eyes. He decided to stop looking at the bright dazzling sky, and to concentrate on something

9

close beside him. There was a bright glint in the sand, brighter than the sparkle of the tiny quartz fragments, and he fixed his eyes upon it.

After a minute he was able to see that he was gazing at a large blue diamond. The sight of it disturbed him because he was sure that it should have been picked up, for it had the appearance of an object of value. He put it in his pocket.

Standing up, he looked more closely at his surroundings, and observed bright green lizards dodging in and out of the tunnels made by the fluting of the columns where they touched the sand. He noticed, also, that the sand seemed to be covered with blue diamonds, resembling that he had picked up.

So far as he could see, sand stretched endlessly on all sides of him, flat but rippled in some places, and in others rising in small hills. There was neither blade of green grass nor twisted tree-trunk in sight. He seated himself on the chipped base of a column, to attempt to work out a plan of escape. The sun would be of no assistance as a guide, for it was still straight above him, as it had been when he first recovered his senses. It seemed, too, to be rather a curious sun, not so bright as the sun of his native land, and surrounded by concentric rings of different colours—rather like a rainbow but more solid, with each ring clearly defined.

It was very difficult to decide which way to go, but he knew that he could not remain where he was as there did not seem to be any water, and the dryness of the sand seemed to exclude any likelihood of a sudden shower.

As he sat wondering how to escape, he grabbed idly at the lizards which ran boldly over his feet, seemingly incurious about his invasion of their domain. They were not frightened of him; when he made a snatch at one of them it would just dodge nimbly out of reach, looking back at him with little bright black eyes before restarting its apparently aimless dash among the broken stones.

Christopher was vaguely irritated, and increased his efforts, telling himself that he was not going to be beaten by a little non-poisonous reptile, only three or four inches in length.

The pursuit of the swift lizards took his mind off his own predicament and he lay down on the sand again, on his stomach. It was surprising that the sand was not really hot, not nearly so hot as it should have been with the perpendicular sun beating down upon it.

In fact, it was no warmer than it had been at home, and there too often the dull sky had been overcast by leaden clouds. However, it was not his affair, to worry about the temperature; his business was to return to town as quickly as he could. If he looked hard enough, there must be water somewhere in spite of the arid appearance of the sand, or else the lizards could not survive. He made a sudden grasp at one of them, which had come up under his chin, and managed to catch it by one of the front legs.

Lucky, he got it by the front and not by the tail. Lizards were reputed to shed their scaly tails if lifted by them; perhaps this was not true; he could also recollect being told that if he picked a guinea-pig up by its tail its eyes would fall out, though that was before he had seen a guinea-pig and discovered for himself that it was a tailless animal. Whatever the truth of the matter was, he felt that he would be a fool to try it on the lizard before he had examined it.

The poor little devil looks uncomfortable, and no wonder, for would you feel very comfortable yourself if you were picked up by one arm, or leg? He moved his fingers to hold it behind the head and inspected it closely. Seen at that range it was not as green as it had appeared while running on the yellow sand; there were all sorts of

11

colours in its hard skin, little lumps, less than the size of grains of sand, of ochre, of red, both crimson and ver- milion, and of deep blue and black. Its little black, pin-head eyes seemed to flicker nervously as it opened its mouth and shot out a slim blue-black tongue, so fast that Christopher could not see it properly.

It did not struggle much as he looked at it, but must have been saving its strength for a final effort, in which it suddenly twisted and wriggled. Christopher closed his hand quickly, thinking he had managed to hold on to it until he saw it running curiously across the sand to the shelter of one of the stone-blocks. All that he held was about an inch and a quarter of tail, which seemed to have come to life of itself, for it jerked convulsively as he opened his hand to examine it, before it lay still across his palm. He felt a faint disgust at the sight of this independent life and threw the tail after the lizard, saying, "Come and collect your property, brother."

He had not settled down to play games with the lizards, but to decide which way he should go to escape from the sand that stretched for miles around him. It did not seem to matter which direction he chose, and he would go towards the sandy hills, trusting to the tailless lizard's chance direction. These hills might hide the oasis he desired, or might prove the correct exit for any who were lost in the desert.

It occurred to him that he might as well make some money from his accident, if he could; he filled one of his pockets with the blue diamonds, wondering at their enormous size and apparent flawlessness, for he could distinguish none of the cracks or marks usually found in crystals.

Perhaps I have been knocked out by some fragment of stone and this is nothing but a dream. He pinched his thigh and his nails, as he decreased the area pinched, drove in deeply to hurt him.

12

He shut one of the blue pebbles in his hand and clenched it tightly, thinking that it might vanish or turn to water like the cheese the boy squeezed when the giant challenged him to crush a stone; but, though he squeezed so hard that he felt as though it would become embedded in his flesh, no change befell it.

As he sauntered towards the low ridge of hills, Christopher wondered what Mr. Pergen would think when he did not turn up for his interview; someone else would presumably get the job, and his mother would be very angry when she heard that he had not turned up at the appointed time; and, as for his father—well, he would talk, in a tight voice, precisely, of gratitude to those who gave away every chance in life, of the need for courtesy to one's elders, and of the value of punctuality.

Perhaps he would be able to plead that he had had an accident and was consequently delayed, but it was most unfair that he should have to be the person to be transported to this blasted desert, on the very afternoon that he was to get the job which, he hoped, would make him independent of his parents.

If he told them he had woken up in the middle of a desert, his father would look at him and murmur about liars, under his breath, and his mother would move closer to him to smell whether he had been drinking. Of course, he could always produce the blue diamonds, which bulged one pocket, but then his parents would look at him as if he was a thief as well as a liar, and they would probably take his treasure from him and give it to the police.

But all this was problematical, depending upon his escape from the desert, which seemed to go on to the world's end. He wondered how he had got into the tangle of ruined villas and temples, for he had seen no footsteps other than his own, and the little bird-like tracks of the lizards in the sand.

It seemed to be taking a long time to reach the hill

13

which quivered ahead of him, quivered without reason, for the sun sent down very little heat from its vertical position in the sky.

Treading the topaz-coloured sand, he noticed that the uncut precious stones had not been confined by the boundaries of the ruined city, but were spread all about the desert. It disturbed him, for these jewels seemed to declare that he was walking in an uninhabited section of country, otherwise the desert would have been scoured by men in caterpillar-wheeled trucks, shovelling up the wealth so fortuitously spread about.

Perhaps he was walking in the wrong direction, with the soft sand shifting beneath his boots, and he would keep on plodding through this dry bog until he fell down, and then he would die. This cold sun would take a long time to strip his bones of flesh, but in the end he would lie there, very little different from any chance mule that had fallen by the wayside.

The hill was neither steep, nor high, and he climbed it easily; but from its summit he saw only another hill shivering a mile or two ahead of him. He went towards it.

The whole affair was rather like one of these Chinese ivory boxes; when you opened it you found another box inside, and so on until you came to the ultimate minute fragment, solid. Here he climbed a hill, and all that he could see ahead of him was another hill; he reached that hill and there was yet another beyond it. He tried to cheer himself by thinking that, even though he might be in a puzzle-box, persistence would find the solid centre; and, for him, that would be the flat plain that led towards the town and home.

In spite of the sand which seemed to wish to impede his steps, he did not feel at all tired, and sauntered slowly from one hill to the next, across the sand which now sparkled with precious stones of all sorts; emeralds, moonstones, turquoises, rubies, amethysts, garnets, opals, cornelians and diamonds.

Although he seemed to have been walking for several hours, the sun still shone directly over his head. He wondered how people told the time; they would need some other method of reckoning than the sun. Having the sun directly above you, perpetually, you could have no night, and no north, no south, neither east nor west; there would be no directions except by landmarks.

Perhaps he was mad and his brain had invented its own landscape and its own sun; perhaps, even now, he was wandering in familiar streets, dazed by the explosion, while people looked at him in the kindly fashion reserved for those who had been stroked by the lightning flash of madness; these hills might be figments of his imagination, and his mind might have been turned outside in, seeing empty space in the crowded streets, and a multitude in the real and actual desert towards which he was going.

No, however, there was no doubt about it. He was as sane as he had ever been, and speculation about his arrival in this strange place was the only thing that might disturb the balance of his mind.

He could not understand why he did not feel hungry or tired, for he seemed to have been travelling for hours, on the wearisome surface of the sand. If, as he suspected, he was near the equator, then it was strange that the sand did not burn and that there was no glare from it; it sparkled and shone but did not blind him in the least. The light, to be sure, was strong enough, but the climate was as gentle as it had been at home.

As he reached the top of the hundredth hill and looked ahead, to see how far away the next one lay, he discovered that he had reached the centre of the puzzle-box, and that a flat stretch ran before him for several miles.

At the end of this plain a rocky ridge rose sharply.

15

There were no more hills to climb, and once he reached the rocks, long slivers set upright in the sand, he would soon be on the savanna, and once there would find a village and ask the shortest way home.

Glancing down at the sand, he noticed that it was no longer rich with jewels, but had become infested with crawling things. He saw ruby-coloured scorpions, and ochre centipedes, moving about their own small activities, and he felt cheered by the sudden appearance of a vast swallowtail butterfly which began dipping about his head, for he knew then that he could not be far from the green lands which he desired.

He was not sure why he wanted them, for, as yet, he felt neither hunger nor thirst nor weariness, and there did not seem to be any reason for him to hurry from the desert. It was, he supposed, the natural fear of a deserted place, a fear of the wilderness, and also the desire to find a spot where he would be able to obtain food, drink and shelter as he needed them.

He put his hand in the pocket of his jacket, and fiddled with the diamonds, hoping that they, at least, would prove the truth of his story and serve to show his father that he was not lying.

He tried to remember the accounts of the principal deserts of the world as given in the geography books at school, and while they seemed to agree fairly well with most of the purely physical aspects of his desert, none had been mentioned where the sun was suspended in a multi-coloured setting, directly overhead.

Of course, near the equator the midday sun *is* perpendicular, but that only at noon. Since he was sure that he was not mad, it would seem improbable that the explosion could have disturbed his sense of time to the extent where he could have moved all this distance in a moment, while the long hand of a clock was steady for the twelve strokes of noon. He must have wandered into some place where the real sun does not shine and that above me is a species of mirage.

Travelling on for a mile or two, he saw ahead of him an avenue of cactus plants and made towards it. The twisted prickly shapes fringed a road paved with blue slate, and he was glad to walk upon the firm surface after the irritating movement of the sand, which seemed to desire to suck him down into its marsh; a peculiar bog where there were no blackened roots of oak or heather, no fleshy marigolds or bog-beans blooming round its verge, and no water to soften its hard dry clutch.

There were bright flowers on the cacti, and they were unexpectedly soft and fragile for the flowers of such hard and brutal plants; plants spiked with subtle little bunches so arranged that if one point missed another penetrated, or with blue gold and scarlet daggers like the flint arrows Christopher had once found when walking on the green downs, hidden in a hollow of chalk, veined like cheese. He had been surprised then to discover the tough core of the soft greenness, and now wondered whether, in return, the centre of all this brittle sharpness would not be as soft and mushy as the flesh of an over-ripened peach.

On the cactus flowers there were butterflies of all sorts and colours, blue, bright lemon-yellow, Indian red, royal purple and a multitude of browns. These butterflies were more or less invisible until he drew level with them, and then they rose in clouds and whirled round his head, like a crowd of sparrows mobbing a rook which had ventured too near the place they claimed as their own property.

Perhaps even now he was walking on Tom Tiddler's Ground, and suddenly the awful face would turn round before him. It would be the famous head which the traveller in far countries brought back with him, the face that turned all who gazed upon it into pillars of stone.

Christopher determined that he would be ready to fling himself face down upon the path, if he detected a move-

17

ment ahead. Then he laughed at his childish fears, telling himself that there was no point in supping trouble with a long spoon.

There was really nothing for him to fear, for his boots would protect him against the only immediate dangers, the stings of the scorpions or the fangs of the small fat puff-adders which he now noticed sliding swiftly away from him towards the sheltering cracks in the slate.

Once he trod on one of these small snakes, not heavily, for he jumped quickly aside as he felt the movement beneath his foot; the snake turned as fast as his eye could follow it, and struck sharply at the leather, but he barely felt it and pushed his assailant gently aside. Looking at the place where the sharp fangs had made impact, he could see two narrow parallel runnels, moist with venom. He went to the side of the track and wiped the boot against a short, stubby cactus, setting up a swarm of small red and yellow flies that darted angrily past him to find a more secure refuge.

Although he might laugh at his fears, and call himself a fool for inventing difficulties and dangers, Christopher was not able to control his physical reaction when something moved a little distance ahead. He threw himself down on the slate path, so hard that, had it been an ordinary day, he would have bruised his hands and his face. He lay absolutely motionless, a little surprised that he had not hurt himself, and waited to see what would happen.

He told himself that the story of the Gorgon's head was only a legend, and one that had been common currency for hundreds of years before his birth, but it took as much courage as he possessed to peer out under his arm.

At first he could see nothing, and thought that the movement he had detected had been an invention of his too eager mind, seeking for something to satisfy its expec-

18

tation of danger, but then he saw, turning slowly on the ground in front of him, the shadow of something that looked like an aeroplane.

He leaped to his feet. It was the plane which had brought him into this desolate place, and now it could jolly well take him out of it. A joke was all right as a joke, but it was taking it a bit too far to dump a man in a desert and leave him there to wander on the rippled plain or among the hillocks, under a tropical sun.

His indignation rose like a fountain before he had time to lift his eyes to look at the plane, which was sending its shadow in circles on the smooth blue slate. He raised his eyes and was horrified to see, instead of the immaculate swift monoplane he expected, a large vulture, hovering on tightly stretched wings, only a few yards above his head. When he moved his arm up, as if to ward off an attack upon his face, it did not take alarm, but merely lifted itself higher into the blue glazed bowl of the sky, in lazy spirals.

Christopher wondered what he could do; he had no weapon, and even if he managed to get over the difficulty of the spines on the cacti and rooted one up, it would not make a satisfactory cudgel. The vulture would sweep it from his hand with one blow of its powerful wings or strong yellow claws.

However, for the moment, it did not seem to wish to attack him and appeared content to float slowly up, and down, and round in the currentless air.

His best plan would be to make for the rocky ridge as fast as he could; there he might find a deep and narrow crevice, where the huge bird would be unable to descend to strike at him.

He tried to hurry, but found that he had only one pace, the one he had been using, and that his legs would not move any faster, even though he kept assuring himself of the necessity for speed. Night might come on suddenly;

the sun be shut out like the lens of a camera when the shutter flashes across it.

He felt as fresh as if he had just risen from a long night's sleep, on a firm yet soft mattress. Glancing back over his shoulder, he saw that the last of the low sand hills was almost out of sight behind him, half-hidden in a haze of shivering blue air.

He remembered having read that vultures did not like to tackle an agile victim, preferring to find one dead, or else weak and unable to resist. However, he recollected also the condor, the vulture of the Andes, supposed to be fearless; he recalled tales of its attacks upon giant air-liners as they flew past its eyrie, perched on some inaccessible ledge. He hoped that he had not been landed somewhere in South America, and that the bird above him was not a condor; he was not able to visualize the name written under the picture which he identified with his unwanted escort.

The vulture, supposing its behaviour to indicate its species, did not seem to be very interested in him, beyond keeping an eye open to see that he did not escape, for, occasionally, it gave a strong sweep of its wings and slid easily away to a distance of a mile or so. There it would swing down towards the earth and examine the ground before it returned to Christopher.

As they went along the road at their different levels, Christopher was disturbed to see that one or two ravens had appeared, as if from the bowels of the desert, and were following the vulture, showing their respect for the giant hawk in the manner in which they scurried aside when his facile swings took him in their direction.

It seemed Christopher was doomed to fall somewhere in the desert, for was it not true that these scavenger birds seldom made a mistake in their choice of victim, never following a man who retained full mastery of his faculties? Therefore, he must even now be weakening, although he

20

did not know it and still felt as fresh as he had all along. He would probably fall quite suddenly, everything would be sudden in this queer country, and then the vulture would come slowly, dropping ever so slowly in contrast to *his* fall. Its talons would be stretched out stiffly towards his recumbent form; it would grip the unresistant flesh and its swift beak would start the task of stripping the flabby meat from the dead body, choosing only the most tender portions. Then would come the ravens, croaking heavily as they pecked out the eyes which would no longer shine like wet pebbles; strutting solemnly like priests around the body which would know no funeral, nor be buried by anything except the movements of the topaz sand as it crept like a tide over the slate slabs. Lastly would come the black ants, and the red ants, and the brown ants, to claim their countless fragments, and then there would be nothing left of him; nothing but some clean bones (hollow nests for scorpions) and an empty skull grinning fatuously at the road which no one ever trod.

Christopher felt sorry for himself as he saw this picture of his remains lying where he was walking now, and it took him a few moments to get control of his emotions and tell himself that he was a fool and could, at least, still make an effort to reach the sanctuary of the strata-ed rocks ahead.

The butterflies on the cacti did not seem to be perturbed by the birds which escorted him; they fluttered about his head, and once or twice flew right into his face. When one of them did this and fell, temporarily stunned, to the path, Christopher decided that he would sacrifice it to see what happened, for he remembered once having seen a rook snatch a butterfly and eat it. The ravens dived down to look at the stunned insect, and for a moment he thought they were going to eat it, quarrelling stiffly over the fragment of life. However, they apparently decided

21

that it was not worth the trouble and flew off, as fast as they could, in pursuit of the vulture.

Still the sun shone bright and cold, and Christopher wondered if he had come to some place where there was perpetual sunlight. It was muddling; worse than imagining himself peering over the farthest brink of space.

As he walked along he took a blue diamond from his pocket and tossed it in the air, catching it as it descended. This trivial action gave him some contact with a reality outside the desert, and he started throwing the bright pebble higher, making slip-catches with one hand. Then he tried with his eyes shut, but he flicked the stone over his back, and he heard it fall on the path behind him.

He turned quickly and bent down to pick it up. As he straightened again he was shocked to see a man throwing something in the air and catching it. Then he realized that he was watching himself, and he knew that he was mad, and turned round as fast as he could.

There was no one ahead of him, and he turned his head slowly and gazed back. There was no one there either, and he thought that the whole affair must have been a sudden brainstorm. He turned right round and looked at the road along which he had come so far. It appeared to be exactly the same, and he took a pace back towards the distant hills. Immediately he saw himself coming forward.

Christopher was really frightened by this occurrence, even though it might only be some phenomenon caused by the immovable sun and the sparkling sand. He thought about it for a moment and took several paces back. The other Christopher was there, doing exactly what he had been doing when he had reached that point upon the road.

Then he realized that he had found the answer to all his questions about the motionless sun. He was in a part of the world which was literally *without time*, where it was perpetually midday; that explained why he had not felt hungry nor weary, for everything that occurred had happened at the same instant. It was only in the mind that things happened in a sequence.

The thought of this timelessness made him feel uncomfortable, and he turned back towards the ridge, sighting on the rocks, telling himself that he would be glad when he got home and escaped from this place where things were beyond his comprehension. He determined that he would not look back again, as the whole business was too large for his mind to grasp, and he might really go mad.

He made his way steadfastly towards the wall of rock which, he hoped, marked the edge of the timeless desert with its vultures and ravens, scorpions and precious stones, and avenues of soft petalled cacti.

CHAPTER TWO

AS he went he concentrated on the ridge ahead of him, and saw that it was composed of grey and black slivers of rock, standing up from the sand, looking as if a strata had slipped sideways. The face was brightened in places by the vivid colours of flowers, giving it the effect of a carefully arranged rockery.

While he was still a good way off he was surprised to find that everything stood out very clearly, and he could identify several of the flowers; there were sea-pinks (what on earth were sea-pinks doing here?), and saxifrages and sedums of all colours, with thick plump leaves tinted a deep plum-purple at the base.

The vulture still hovered above Christopher's head, but he was playing a game with himself, pretending that it was not polite to notice his escort. He realized that, if it made a sudden dive at him all he had to do was to step back hurriedly, and he would really be back before it dived; the only trouble about this solution was that it would then be rather difficult to go forward as the vulture would be there waiting for him. What he would have to do, he thought, would be to try to dodge it in space by travelling sideways, and not returning to the same place as before; this might defeat the vulture, but would probably have a bad effect on his own mind, for he certainly had not been designed to manœuvre in space without the help of time.

The whole thing was puzzling indeed, and he told himself that the sooner (but was there any sooner or later?) he got out of this place, and managed to get home, the better he would be pleased. Fortunately, the vulture seemed to be content to drift along above him, turning every now and again to frighten the ravens when they pressed on too fast. The absence of any sort of time did not seem to worry either the birds, or the things that crawled and slithered on the slate path.

The ridge was close at hand, and Christopher counted the cactus-plants that led to it. These plants were placed on either side of the track, some distance apart. There were only seven of them, and he walked towards the first, thinking that he could use them as a mental tight-rope to pull himself towards the rocks, and feeling glad that he had found something stable in the shifting timelessness of the desert.

The first cactus was a tall hexagonal column of dark green; spines arranged in couples along the angles, dark brown at base lightening to a sandy yellow at the sharp tips. It had a large dark mauve flower, which looked rather like a single bloom picked from a hollyhock and pinned on the alien plant. A large orange and black beetle with strong antlers was walking up it, towards a small powder-blue butterfly; whenever it got near the butterfly moved

24

on a foot or so and the beetle had to start stalking again. Christopher wondered vaguely what would happen when they reached the top, but did not wait to see.

The second was composed of large flat ovals, with little hair-like thorns in bunches of about thirty, and was free of any flower. Earwigs, small and brown and hard, ran in between the little copses of spikes, and encountered one another with sufficient force to knock them off. When this happened, they did not fall to the ground, but opened transparent wings, hidden in hard cases, and came back to the place where they had been. They remained facing one another, folding their wings carefully with their feet, until one made way for the other.

The third cactus was composed of globes stuck one on top of the other, with long black thorns sticking out at random over them. A bee buzzed noisily in the single giant orange flower, and Christopher knew that he must be approaching the edge of the desert, for the bee would require more than the flowers of a few cacti or dry rock plants.

The first cactus was repeated in miniature by the fourth, but the flower was lacking. The fifth had vast green sores that exuded a stench like that of decaying meat. Pale olive-green maggots fed on the crusted edges of these sores, and irridescent bluebottles fussed around, laying clutches of eggs which were immediately devoured by the maggots. The sixth was hollow in the centre and contained a pool of gluey amber liquid, like amber in more than its colour, for it held, preserved, the bodies of several insects, ants, butterflies, moths and beetles.

The last cactus of all was a thin straggling one, looking rather like a stick-insect; it was the home of all sorts of spiders, and their webs, thick as silk or thin as the finest hair, were suspended all over it. There was no gap between the twigs that was not webbed perfectly; no insect had been trapped to break the symmetry of any. All the

25

spiders were crouched on tight lines that would act as alarms if a fly did chance to stumble into any web. They were big as pennies and smaller than pin-heads; coated in black velvet and lacquered, red vulcanite or blue as turquoises and green as lovebirds. Under the cactus sat a large toad, brown and olive warted skin, his throat swelling and collapsing as he breathed, waiting, apparently, for some morsel to slip from one of the webs. Beside the toad there coiled a little coral snake, which raised its head and darted a damp black tongue as Christopher approached.

Perhaps the most curious thing about the cactus was that the ground beneath it was scattered with white flowers, looking as if they had just fallen from it, though Christopher could see no signs of their having been attached to the plant.

He stooped, being careful to keep well away from the coral snake, and picked up one of the flowers to examine it more closely. Inside the petals lay a ladybird, seven white spots on its scarlet shell; he looked at other flowers to see what they contained—each held a similar ladybird. He shook one of them out into his hand, expecting it to crawl across his hand, but it lay still and was curiously heavy. He found, when he turned it over, that it was not a real insect at all, but a cunning counterfeit in bronze, painted so skilfully that it needed a close inspection to discover that it was not living and asleep.

He shook the ladybirds out of several flowers and discovered that they were all of bronze. As he removed an insect he threw the flower down; stooping to pick up another he noticed that those he had robbed had shrivelled into brown dry tobacco-twists, like leaves in winter.

This was certainly strange, for it was not his handling that had perished the flowers; when he held one in his cupped hand for a moment, but did not remove the

26

insect, it remained firm and crisp as a gardenia, when he removed the ladybird it shrivelled immediately.

He thought that this was the work of man, but, granting that, he could not understand why the flowers should be affected by the bronze ladybirds, nor, indeed, how they came to be there at all, for they did not seem to have fallen from the spider-infested cactus. Yet there was no other possible source, for the nearest flowers were those on the ridge, still a quarter of a mile distant, and there was no wind to transport them, or group them carefully around the base of one cactus. He looked at the sifting of sand on the slate road but could see nothing except the scrawled marks where the scorpions had scurried, and the shallow ruts dug by the bodies of the puff-adders as they slithered about.

Of course, it was such a queer country that anything might happen, and the flowers might have been there for centuries (there was no measure for their endurance), and the steps of the man who had placed them there might have been obliterated by the continual passing of the desert creatures. He collected a few of the bronze ladybirds and put them in his breast-pocket, thinking that they would be something more to show to prove the truth of his tale.

It really was rather worrying, this absence of time, for it meant that, at home, time had been going on as usual, and he might have been away for years and have been given up for lost; on the other hand, he might only have been gone five minutes, and they would wonder what he was talking about when he told them the story of his wanderings; would think that there was something evil in the blue diamonds, the rubies, the emeralds and the bronze ladybirds.

It was strange the way in which he clung to the common usage of temporal phrases—he told himself *it was time* he settled the affair. It was almost impossible to live with-

27

out these phrases, or without time, and it made him realize how much his whole life had depended upon the ticking of a clock.

As he drew near to the ridge another danger presented itself, for he had decided that the ridge was the verge of the timeless desert. He began to fear that he might be a prisoner of timelessness, and so would not be able to reach the safety-zone of time. Perhaps he had been in the desert for such a 'long time,' judged by normal standards, that he would immediately die of old age if he managed to get out.

All this time, or space, he had been approaching the wall of rock, casting glances along it to see if he would be able to climb out easily. Now he saw, straight ahead of him, a crack between two pillars.

He stood at the entrance to the shady crevice, looking back at the desert, which did not seem to look extra-ordinary in retrospect. The flat sand rose into hills in the distance, and there were ripples on its surface, like the seashore on a calm day, when little tongues of water had merely curled lazily up the beach.

The vulture had landed and now sat, its wings folded, about a hundred yards back, with the two blue-black ravens some distance from it to show their respect for the food finder.

At least, I have managed to escape from these beastly carnage eaters, and have reached the rocks in safety, though, perhaps, my fears were vain, as hunger cannot be a strong motive in a timeless place. " Now," he said, "for the path back to sanity."

He went into the rocky gully, noticing at once that the landscape had an air of normality. He could not place this faint flavour for a moment or two, and then realized, with inexpressible relief, that the cause lay in the sun. No longer a globe surrounded by belts of bright colour, hung above his head, but a white mass, low to his left, lay above the horizon. He had returned to a country where there were still hours and minutes, years and days, and he had not become an old man during the transition.

He took the precious stones out of his pockets, quite expecting to find that they had become lumps of mud or dung, but they still retained their appearance of genuineness, and the ladybirds were still bronze and had not come to life with the return to normality.

Now that he was safe he felt a little tired, and more than a little hungry, but he did not dare to stop and seek for berries on the rock-plants, for he was still afraid that he might be swept back into the desert, and forced to wander there for ever, an eternity contained in an instant.

He hurried down the gully, barely glancing at the fragile yellow of the rock-roses and the white and red heads of the sea-pinks, stumbling among the boulders till he reached a place where it was damp and dark; so different from the entrance that he could hardly believe that he had left the desert only a few minutes before.

The walls were steep and trickles of water ran down the cracks, moistening the fibrous roots of ferns, hart's tongue, royal and maiden-hair. The floor was still rocky in parts, but moss covered the rocks and tufty grass made lumps like green stones. A few yards ahead he saw a patch of flat grass, broken by the straggling branches of heather, and approached it cautiously, as if half afraid that it might vanish beneath his feet.

Among the heather he saw the small green and red leaves of a blaeberry plant and, stooping, found the small fruit were ripe, bloomed like black grapes. He took a drink from one of the trickles of water, cupping his hands beneath its coolness, and thought he had never tasted water so delicious. Then he set to work on the blaeberries, smearing his face with their deep crimson juice as he ate.

The plant stripped, he thought he would seek some

place to sleep, but was still frightened by the notion that he might wake to find himself back in the ruined city where he had started. The result was that, although he found several fairly comfortable and dry places, he had no sooner laid himself down and closed his eyes before he was back on his feet, plunging down the gully, away from the nightmare desert.

Now there were animals in the gully; animals that he knew, such as hares and rabbits. He really had escaped from the hard-coated insects and reptiles, and here the birds were no longer carrion seekers, but finches that lived on seeds, or an occasional swallow that dipped after invisible gnats.

Trampling beside a clump of rushes, he startled a snipe which zig-zagged away in a scurry of precise wings. A large dragonfly hovered for a second before his face before darting off sideways, and he saw caterpillars, striped like little tigers, crawling up the stem of a yellow ragwort.

This was the country that he understood, and he was glad that the desert led out into it, and not into some hot eastern land which would have given him an alien feeling. But, in spite of the comfort of familiar country, he was disturbed, remembering the distance that separated his home from such a landscape.

He had no money in his pockets, but once he reached a town he could sell one of his jewels and pay his fare home.

Doubtless there had been some jiggery-pokery, and he was the victim of a plot intended for another. He wondered what the conspirators would think when they realized that it was the wrong man they had marooned. They must have been cunning to dump him in the midst of timelessness and to escape themselves. Presumably they were the master-criminals of the thrillers, who had the services of brilliant scientists, kinked, at their com-

30

mand. Science, he assumed, had found some measure to take the place of time, to enable those who knew to travel without inconvenience in the desert. It was obvious that these crooks could not be driven by desire for riches, for the desert would have made them rich; perhaps the Holy Grail they sought was power, an abstract ideal.

Christopher felt pleased with his explanation of his predicament, and, as he sauntered down the gully, determined, once he reached home, to expose the machinations of the group.

It was beginning to get dark, and the sun, the actual, moving sun, was merely a segment on the horizon. Christopher looked among the stalks of bracken at the track side until he found a flat place, which he covered with heather and fern to make a bed. He knew now that he had escaped from the desert, but determined to take some precaution in case he was sought, so, breaking a thickly foliaged branch from a hazel-bush, he fixed it above his bed to hide him from the air.

Darkness had now fallen, and he heard an owl calling and saw its shape as it glided down from some ledge of the rocks above him. Grasshoppers kept up a continual monotonous drone, to soothe him into sleep.

He did not wake until the sun was well up in the sky. For a moment he did not realize where he was, nor why he was there. Then he pulled on his jacket and washed his face under one of the trickles of water, thankful that he was out of the desert and that the day appeared to be set fair. He breakfasted off a raw horse-mushroom, large as a dinner-plate, which he found on the smooth grass, and then picked more of the acid but refreshing blaeberries.

He broke off a thick stick of hazel, carefully severing the adhesive bark with a sharp splinter of rock to prevent it stripping off. He managed to round the rough end by rubbing it against a stone, and then started off again, down the long gully.

31

Now he was on his way home, and nothing that his parents could say to express their disbelief could alter the truth of his story. He was no longer in any hurry, for, having escaped from the desert, he did not mind when he reached his home. It was now simply a matter of finding a town or a village and asking where he was, and then a swift train journey would finish his adventure.

The gully seemed to be full of birds, and Christopher tried to check the different species, but soon lost count. He saw a golden-crested wren dodging among the branches of a hazel-bush, and a hawfinch on a maythorn, a woodcock sprang startled before him, and the distance was filled with the desolate crying of curlews. The plants were common to the type of country, sundew, pink tinged green and sticky, spotted violet bee-orchis and yellow-starred St. John's wort. At any rate, there was little strange about the natural history of the place, except that the seasons seemed to have become mixed, and the plants and birds were certainly those of his own country.

He wondered about the length of the gully, and hoped that he was not to find it more difficult to escape from this section of the normal than he had from the abnormal. He walked easily, troubled only by his wishes for a cigarette, picking brambles from the bushes that fringed the track. The grass was flat and worn where he walked, showing clearly that it was a track, and one used by men. It was not the trail of an animal, being unmarked by the round pellets of a rabbit's droppings, or the grape-like bunches that showed a sheep had passed that way.

All day he walked, unhurried, and it was towards nightfall that he reached the end of the glen. Ahead of him, as he skirted the last buttress of rock, he saw the outskirts of a city, the houses looking very clean in the long rays of the setting sun and free from the usual pall of smoke above them.

He smoothed his hair down with water and tried to

scrape the dirt from his finger nails with a broken hazel-twig.

Then he set off towards the town, which appeared to be large. The clearness of the evening air had been deceptive, for the apparent distance of a mile or so was, in reality, very much farther. He walked on springy turf of the sort which he associated with golf-courses beside the sea; there were, however, no signs of the ocean, except for a few plants, a silver-leaved creeper among pebbles and blue sea-holly in a sandy hollow, fringed by tough wiry bents. The sun was sinking over the land, and so far as his eye ranged, it caught nothing but this smooth expanse of turf.

As he walked it became darker and no lights sprang out of the windows of the houses, or brightened the streets. It did not have the look of a deserted city, and yet there was something very strange about it, an air of unreality as if it had been made of cardboard and was waiting for a gale to demolish it. It might even be a stage-set, erected for a few performances only. There was certainly something wrong, even though he could not place it; something missing beside chimneys and a cloud of smoke.

When he reached the first house it was practically dark. He found that it was not the small suburban dwelling he had imagined, but a vast block of flats. None of the windows were lighted, and no arc-lamps glared to make the streets a safe place. However, no people walked these streets, and no traffic ran. At the first glance it appeared a dead town. Then Christopher noticed a red glow in the gutter. It was a smouldering cigarette, one that had been lighted recently.

He picked up the cigarette and puffed at it, thinking that they (the mysterious *they* who haunted all his dreams) were playing some game with him. He steadied himself to greet them casually, unstartled by their sudden "Boo."

33

He lounged nonchalantly in a corner, so that they would not catch him unaware.

If they were playing some game it was a strange one, for he saw no one, though he remained standing for ten minutes. Then, irritated, he shouted to them to come out and show themselves, for, though he could take a joke with the best of them, he saw limits to this sort of fun. No one answered him, and he worked his way round to the front door of the flat, to ring and see who answered.

When he got there he found that it was not a real door at all, but merely a shape painted on a smooth concrete wall. Going to the windows, with the intention of breaking in, he found that they also were mere outlines in paint.

This was unlike any town he had known; he tried the next block of flats, and the next, but all were the same, solid concrete without entrance or exit. He knew that there were people in the town, for going round a corner he found another cigarette on the edge of the pavement, newly lighted. From this, he deduced that the citizens of the town might be unwilling to show themselves, but they were not hostile, for these cigarettes could only be meant for him.

He wondered how they had heard of his approach, and how they had guessed that he would desire a cigarette. It was all very disturbing, he decided, walking on into the town; the action of leaving lighted cigarettes in his path might be meant kindly, but, all the same, he would rather see one of the inhabitants than merely be the recipient of their bounty.

There might, he hoped, be some crack in the structure of the city through which he could worm to discover the people. He was quite harmless, and it was strange that his presence should send a whole city into hiding. Several times he thought he saw a movement at a corner ahead

34

of him, but when he reached it and looked down the dark streets, he could see no one.

It was annoying to have to walk so far on these hard pavements after his day's journey. There did not seem to be any shops in the streets, which were, apparently, composed of identical blocks of flats, getting higher as he penetrated farther into the town. Though he tried the doors as he passed them, he found they were merely painted symbols, with neither locks nor handles.

He wondered how the inhabitants managed to get into their homes and what they did for light, but decided against speculation, in the expectation that the farce could not continue for ever and that soon they would show themselves, even if it was only to ask him to leave their town. Several times, in spite of his determination to show no curiosity, Christopher walked right round one of these blocks, to see if he could find a back entrance, but found none.

As he turned a corner he saw, a long way ahead of him, the faint glow of a light. At last, he thought, they have made up their minds to play ball with me. All I have to do is to make for that glare and I will find someone waiting to accost me. It seems to be a strange way to welcome a benighted traveller, but may be the custom in this country; though that is not a reassuring thought, seeming to indicate that I have passed from one queerness to another, by way of a normal belt.

It occurred to him that it might be a trap to lead him into an ambush in the centre of the town, and the kindly action of placing lighted cigarettes in his path might be a sort of ground-bait. He went very slowly, keeping his eyes open and his hearing acute for any sign or sound of treachery. The light seemed to proceed from an open space at the end of a long avenue. This opening, he found, was a great square, floodlit till nearly as light as day.

Christopher noticed that it was filled with statues of

all sorts and sizes, like the yard of a maker of tombstones. There were men on horseback, women recumbent and women posed like ballet-dancers, dolphins, sea-horses, lions, children and groups of elderly, toga-ed city fathers; but all of them were disturbing. They were bleeding from wounds in various parts of the body, and not at one uniform rate, but gushing, dripping or trickling as the size of the wound, and its position, indicated.

Of course, he told himself, it's all just a trick with coloured liquids and fountains, but rather disgusting and pointless. The blood was caught in little lead basins fixed to each figure, and the drainage was so regulated that these basins seemed to be on the point of overflowing. Christopher stuck his finger into one of these pools and smelled it; it *did* smell like blood—and it tasted like it, too; but it could not, he invoked the laws of nature, be real blood, and stone statues could not really bleed.

All his senses revolted against the idea of lead, marble, bronze, alabaster or limestone bleeding; the variety of substances precluded the possibility of one material having an issue of blood-like fluid.

Suddenly Christopher noticed that the square was filled with thousands of pigeons, strutting about the tessellated pavement. He saw one of them pause on the brink of a blood-filled basin and dip its beak; the idea of the birds drinking the blood of statues made him feel rather sick.

Then he saw that the crowd of pigeons was thickest in one particular spot. In the middle of this horde of birds there stood a man. He was tall and thin, with straggling long grey hair, and a long beard, dressed in a leather doublet and knee-breeches.

He seemed to be feeding the pigeons. The sight of a man in this strange gathering cheered Christopher, who went slowly towards the gaunt figure, a figure resembling one of Daumier's paintings of Don Quixote, or something from an etching by Goya. He walked round the statues,

36

thinking that he would see what the man was doing before he spoke.

His approach unheeded, Christopher walked round a sphinx made of pale green Connemara marble. The man certainly was feeding the pigeons, for he had a large sack of grain beside him into which he occasionally dipped his hand, but it was the main part of his activity which immobilized Christopher.

As they came within reach he was catching the pigeons and breaking their necks with a skilful twist of nimble hands. He threw the bodies, still quivering, over his shoulder on to a huge heap of dead birds behind him.

Christopher could not move for a moment, and then he approached the bird-killer, scattering the pigeons with his feet. They did not seem to mind him, but scurried back into the places he cleared, seeking the grains which their destroyer had spread about the ground.

The man did not hesitate in his carnage as Christopher drew near, but continued killing the birds and throwing them over his shoulder, so fast that it seemed to be one continuous movement. He looked at Christopher with pale blue eyes that shone mildly under bushy grey eyebrows.

Christopher found that he was farther from the man then he had imagined, and thought that something must have gone wrong with his eye for distance during his stay in the desert, for this was neither the first nor the second time that he had been misled.

Looking down, Christopher realized that there was a mosaic on the pavement of the square; he swept some of the pigeons aside with his foot and examined the representations. They showed enormous pigeons of all kinds —there was the halo-ed holy dove, the long extinct carrier pigeon, the turtle dove, the rock and wood pigeons, pouters and fantails.

He felt that pigeons must possess some sort of religious

significance for the inhabitants, and that the old man was probably engaged in some deep ritual which demanded that so many pigeons should be slaughtered on a certain date, without the spilling of blood, and that, also, they should be fed before the killing. If it was something like this it would explain why Christopher had not seen any of the inhabitants who, no doubt, were forbidden to show themselves while the monthly, or whatever it was, pigeon-killing was in progress.

The old man kept his eyes fixed on Christopher, who was unable to decide whether they conveyed an invitation or a rebuff, as his murdering hands made no gesture. These long thin hands were terrifying in their precision; when they reached out towards a pigeon they never missed, and made a neat job of the actual killing, their action as regular as a metronome.

Christopher found that his feet kept step with the movements of these hands, and was irritated to discover that they had hypnotized him. He felt slightly frightened, but was unwilling to turn and run, and kept on towards the old man.

Six feet from the man he stopped and pulled himself erect. In a voice as near as normal as he could manage, he asked, "Why are you killing the doves?"

The old man did not reply, but flicked the corpse he held over his shoulder, and Christopher asked again, "Why do you kill the birds?"

Still there was no answer, and Christopher, deciding that the old man was deaf, gathered his breath to shout his question a third time. Before he expelled the words, however, the bird-killer spoke in a soft dreamy voice. "Blood for the statues," he said, "blood for the statues."

He did not pause in his work, and Christopher, his question answered, turned his back and went towards the shadows of the bleeding statues.

38

CHAPTER THREE

As he entered the dark shadow of a statue of justice, Christopher heard the deep tolling of a bell and saw two men in front of him. Their clothes appeared strange to him; they wore bright helmets, adorned with the wings of a hawk, white tunics that came down to within a few inches of their knees; their calves were encased in brass greaves, and their feet were shod in leather sandals. One of them carried a violin, the other a naked sword.

Christopher was startled and stopped dead. They were angels, and the sight of them could only have one meaning.

So," he gasped, "I'm dead. I never thought it would be like this."

Both the men hooted with laughter, and the sword-bearer jabbed Christopher in the ribs with the point of his weapon. "Don't feel very dead, do you, eh?" he enquired. "You just wait. What are you doing out at this time of night? Why don't you obey orders?"

"Who are you?" Christopher was slightly imperious. "And to what orders do you refer? I am a stranger just come to your town, who can find none to greet him."

The man with the violin drew the bow across the strings, and Christopher watched the shadows round him become alive with men, all dressed in the same fashion as his original interlocutors. The violinist spoke, "We are the night-watchmen, and it is our duty to stop travellers after nightfall. When the curfew rings none may travel without a permit from *Him*. What are you going to do?"

Christopher had not the slightest idea what he was going to do, and told them that his future behaviour depended upon them; he was sorry to have broken the law, but, after all, they should have made some provision for the reception of strangers.

The men gathered in a huddle, like American footballers discussing a piece of strategy before the kick-off, then one of them, who carried a silver rod, cast in imitation of Mercury's staff with a snake and wings, came forward and struck an attitude.

"Stranger," he intoned, "you have broken our laws, but have done so unwittingly. It has been said that ignorance is no defence, but, as *He* is both merciful and reasonable, I am sure that *He* would want us to receive you as you would have been received during the hours of daylight—had that been possible. However, it is not possible, for, as you will see, it is not daylight now. The best I can do for you is to keep you for the night and then, early in the morning, you will be told about your future deportment."

Four watchmen, apparently of lower rank, walked forward and seized Christopher's arms, two to each arm, as if they were afraid that he would make a dash for freedom, and the man with the silver rod advanced, taking a broad strip of leather from a pouch at his belt. With this he bound Christopher's eyes.

It was useless to try and remember which way they walked, for at odd intervals his captors twirled Christopher round and round so that he became dizzy. After they had walked for some time he heard a door clang shut behind him. They went along a corridor, their footsteps echoing damply, and turned several corners before they came to a stop, and the bandage was removed.

He was in a small square room, small, at least, as to the ground-plan, though it was so high that perspective made the ceiling look as though it was only a quarter of the

40

size of the floor. A large man, wearing a suit of leather cut so skilfully that it might have been the finest tweed, sat on a tall three-legged stool, playing with a bunch of flowers. He took a dog-daisy from the bunch and started pulling the petals from it, muttering to himself. His actions were so slow and precise that Christopher felt that each white petal took about a minute on its fluttering descent to the floor, which was strewn with the petals of other flowers, red poppies, marigolds, geraniums, and roses.

The man in leather finished his destructive task and looked at Christopher. "You're lucky!" he exclaimed in a very high voice. "You're too lucky. Take him down, take him down!"

He seemed to be disappointed, and Christopher was just about to question him when the watchmen took control and whirled him out of the room by another door. They went along a long corridor until they came to a slope. There they paused, and the man with the silver rod addressed Christopher, "Keep on down this slope until you reach the end. Wait there till you receive your orders in the morning." He stopped and stared at Christopher with yellow eyes like those of a cat. "I wouldn't advise you to try moving before you get your orders." His voice sounded as though he meant a great deal more than the pure words conveyed.

Christopher started off down the slope and discovered that he was on a great spiral, getting narrower as he descended. He looked back and was pleased to note that none of the night-watchmen were following him, although they might still be at the entrance to the incline. He was glad that he was alone once more, for they had made him feel rather uncomfortable. The frank looks on their faces had been belied by the mystery of their words.

One thing for which he was grateful was the fact that the passage was very well lighted. This lighting seemed to come from the walls, but they were certainly not made of glass, and felt as though they were ordinary concrete.

The floor was of rubber, and Christopher's boots made no clatter as he walked, but he was disturbed to notice, when he turned back, that he had left footprints impressed in the rubber, as if he had been walking on newly-laid cement. He stooped and bent down to look at one of his tracks, and realized that the rubber was gradually becoming smooth again; he heard a sort of sigh as, at last, it showed a surface as smooth as that in front of him.

It seemed strange to pave floors with this soft material, but, he supposed, there was some reason for it; perhaps the rubber would act as an alarm when he walked, and so tell the watchers that he had not turned back.

The decline seemed to continue indefinitely, even after it had become quite a small spiral, and Christopher began to feel dizzy. As it had descended the incline had become steeper, and he was now moving so fast that, if he had been on level ground, he would have been spinning like a top.

Suddenly he came to a drop, and he was travelling at such speed that he could not stop but fell right over the edge. As he fell he thought resentfully of the trick which had been played upon him.

However, he landed so softly that he would not have believed he had fallen at all if he had not seen the end of the passage, thirty feet above him, closing like a toothless mouth.

He was in a curious cell, rather like those that are supposed to be found in lunatic asylums, with a springy floor of soft rubber and walls apparently made of the same material, lighted from the ceiling. There was a carafe of water in a corner and a bowl of fruit. He thought for a moment before he took a plum, afraid that it might be drugged, but he examined it carefully and detected no puncture, such as would have been left by a hypodermic syringe. He ate well, washing the fruit down with draughts of the water, which was lime-flavoured.

After his day's journey he was tired, and dazed by his recent treatment. He could not decide whether the watchmen had been friendly or antagonistic towards him. He lay down on the soft floor and took a last look round his cell. There was no sign now of the hole through which he had entered; it was completely closed, and rubber seemed to have fused over the aperture.

The air in his cell was fresh, though he saw no fans or other ventilating arrangements. Anyhow, they did not mean to kill him outright, and were making him fairly comfortable.

Christopher decided that he would spend some time in the morning, once he got free, in exploring the town, to find the reason for the windowless and doorless houses. It should not prove difficult to make the watchmen understand that he had not meant to flaunt their laws, and that he was a genuine traveller who had transgressed by accident. Presumably, once he found his way about the city, he would manage to learn where the shopping centre was situated and be able to sell one or two of his precious stones.

It seemed to Christopher that he had no sooner fallen asleep before he was woken by a shrill whistle. He sat up and looked around him, but could see no one. Then there was a voice which seemed to come from all parts of the room at the same time.

"In five minutes," it said, "a door will open and, by *His* orders, you will go through that door and walk along the passage. This will lead you right out into the country, and *He* hopes that, when you get there, you will return to the city by daylight, arriving at a decent and conventional time, and that you will not trouble *Him* or *His* watchmen again. Your needs will be attended to upon your return. Be careful, however, for though *He* is merciful, *He* will not countenance the man who errs twice, even though it be through ignorance."

Christopher took another drink of water and ate more fruit. When he had finished he glanced round him and saw that the rubber walls were puckering and wrinkling in one place. He went towards it and waited. Gradually a hole opened and grew bigger until it was large enough to admit his body.

As he squeezed through the aperture, Christopher examined the edges carefully to see if there was some cunning arrangement of steel plates to produce the effect of rubber being sucked apart, but he found neither plates nor wires, and the rubber edges were flexible and elastic. If he had known about it the previous night, he could probably have broken his way out, breaking the carafe and using a fragment as a trowel with which to dig.

It was a queer idea to send him out into the country again, but if it was one of the local bye-laws and not merely a victimization of himself, it was not worth fighting against it. Since there did not seem to be any chance of accelerating his departure for home, an extra day or two spent wandering in the country would not matter. It was pretty obvious that he was in a foreign country, for his countrymen did not dress in such a strange fashion, nor would they have tolerated a square of statues flowing pigeon's blood. These people, and their superstitions, were still of a savage type; they had not reached a normal level of civilization, in spite of all their cunning gadgets.

Christopher wondered about the personage whom they referred to as *He* or *Him*, giving him capitals by their pronunciation of the pronoun. *He* seemed to be the ruler of the state, but it was strange that they did not call *Him*, His Royal Highness, perhaps, or His Excellency, or something like that. The way in which they reverenced their ruler, as if he was a major god, made Christopher feel rather uncomfortable.

The corridor in which he found himself was much the same as the one he had descended the previous night, except for the fact that it was straight. After he had walked along about a hundred yards the floor started to move and, realizing that he was on an escalator, he sat down.

He looked at his precious stones, calculating that he had sufficient to bring him in a few hundred pounds a year once he had sold them and invested the proceeds. He would travel only in nice normal places for the future, keeping well away from deserts and unknown cities. He rolled the bronze ladybirds round the palm of his hand, thinking that he would have them made up into cuff-links.

Undoubtedly he still had difficulties to surmount before he left the country, as he had no identity papers with which to satisfy frontier officials. He would certainly need to find where his consul lived, and attempt to obtain an interim passport, and an advance to pay his passage home.

Though the escalator was moving fast, faster than his ordinary walking pace, it was taking a very long time to get outside the city walls. Surely the beastly thing was not taking him back to the desert—that really would be too much; if that happened he certainly would not return to the city, but would strike off in another direction, in search of a more normal township, where the statues in the public square were more conventional.

As he remembered the pigeons, Christopher thought it curious that the largest of his rubies was of that deep colour known as 'pigeon's blood,' and he wondered whether it was not, perhaps, an evil token which had led him to this place. It might be, on the other hand, that it was a talisman, his good fortune in a single stone, and accounted for the gentle treatment which he had had from the night-watchmen.

At last the escalator slowed down, and Christopher rose and walked up the passage into the open air. He came out in the middle of a copse of hazel bushes and stood, dazed by daylight, for half a minute.

When he turned to take a last look at the tunnel which had brought him to this place, he found that its mouth had completely vanished, leaving no mark upon the ground. It could not have disappeared utterly, for, after all, it was a man-made thing, but when he tried the ground he found that it was no matter of rubber camouflage, but just ordinary leaf mould covered with common wood plants, jack-in-the-pulpit and wood-sorrel.

The entrance to the tunnel might never have been there, and the plants were real plants, with real sap in their stems, sap which left green and brown stains on his fingers when he squeezed it out.

He set off in the direction from which he guessed that he had come, breaking his way through the thick branches of the hazel bushes, and pulling his trousers free from the snarls of bramble which hooked on to them. His jacket became covered with burrs, both big and small, and he stopped to pull them off in case any should get into his hair; remembering once, as a small boy, his fall against a burdock, and his mother removing the barbed things, tugging till it hurt. As he went he startled blackbirds, and they flew away protesting at the way he had invaded their home.

It seemed to be quite a large coppice, and someone had, at some time or other, intended to turn it into a plantation, for he saw rows of stunted firs and larches, tipped pale green, as he pushed through. Once he nearly trod on a pheasant, which whirled up into the sky, in both appearance and noise resembling a Catherine wheel which had broken loose from its stick.

Finally, however, he stood on the edge of an expanse of grass and looked out towards the city. He could scarcely believe his eyes, and was half convinced that he had made a mistake, for the city he was looking at was not the one he had seen at sundown the day before. That had been an affair of concrete buildings that resembled boxes, increasing in height towards the centre of the city, while this was a most peculiar mixture of all sorts of Gothic and baroque revival architecture, arranged in the most higgeldy-piggeldy manner imaginable.

It was built of red and yellow brick, crowned with useless things, stone eagles perched on the top of minute villas, an electric power station, or some such building, possessed a chimney which was the replica of a cathedral tower, complete to the elaborate carving and the gargoyles.

Yet, in spite of the dissimilarity, Christopher knew that it must be the same town, for no other had been visible from the ridge; he supposed there was some illusionary trick at work—perhaps, for instance, the city looked functional from one approach and Gothic from another. It was disturbing, however, to leave a place with one appearance and, on one's return, to find that appearance totally different; but it was no use wondering, while *His* anger was still untested and problematical.

The city might have looked as though it was only a quarter of a mile away, for each of the pinnacles on the chimney was as sharp and clear as if engraved against the sky, and the lines of mortar between the bricks showed up as clearly as in a scale drawing, but he found that eight hundred paces did not decrease the apparent distance by any appreciable amount.

Time in this place might run according to plan, but he could not say the same for their ideas of space. It had become common for him to find that things were really far off when they looked almost at his finger-tips. Even if there was something wrong with space it was not a logical wrongness, like the absence of time in the desert, for sometimes the eye did not deceive.

It might be that *He* had some control over things like that, and was trying to regulate Christopher's approach so that he would not reach the city until it suited *Him*.

Christopher wondered what his father and mother would be thinking. He had never been a particularly dutiful or obedient son, and he had quarrelled often with his parents, but now he felt himself growing quite sentimental as he thought of their worry, and he hoped that the city enjoyed the mechanical blessings of the civilization he had left, to enable him to wire them and put their minds at ease. Thank God he had the jewels and the night-watchmen had not searched him and taken them away, for now he could not expect the job which Mr. Pergen had promised him; Mr. Pergen would talk about dependability, and hum, and haw, and then say that he was sorry but the post had been filled, and there did not seem to be any likelihood of another vacancy in the near future.

The city advanced and retreated; just a moment before he could have sworn that he was gaining on it, and now it was as far away and unattainable as ever. Suddenly, from somewhere in the centre of the town, a huge balloon, with floppy ears like those of a Belgian hare, shot up into the sky.

It discharged a shower of green and purple lights, like Bengal matches, and, from a maroon hidden on board, expelled a blast of sound which nearly knocked Christopher over.

The city was no longer the Gothic higgeldy-piggeldy jumble, but the well-designed structure of flats. There was something the matter with his eyesight, he told himself, for these things could not happen. The town had had real

48

houses, however odd, with real windows, only a few moments before, and now he was inspecting a mass of these beastly shells, without doors or windows, which had helped to depress him the previous night. Of course, there was trickery somewhere, but it did not seem to be very courteous to play these jokes on a stranger, particularly one whom you had invited to return to your city.

The balloon was still there, and seemed to be drifting towards him. If it was responsible for these pranks, Christopher was damned if he was willing to be placated by any approaches it made. He would cut it dead when it came near, and would ignore their hails of welcome, showing them that he was not the man to be trifled with by some pipsqueak civic dignitaries with a schoolboy sense of humour.

He worked himself into a state where, indignantly, he would have rejected the hand of friendship had it been held out to him. However, the balloon was making no attempt to parley with him, but merely sailed round him once or twice, distantly, as if inspecting him, and the maroon tootled again gently.

Christopher did not look at the airship. He was being snooty and would not admit its presence. After all, two can play these games and, if the commander of the balloon thought he was being funny, he would soon be shown the puerility of his jokes.

Keeping his eyes fixed upon the square boxes that made up the city, Christopher suddenly saw them slide down to reveal the Gothic mixture as before. He realized that these walls must divide the city into sections, so that no stranger would be able to penetrate beyond the appearance of the benighted town. He was not very astonished, and felt quite pleased with himself for having guessed that it was a conjuring trick. All the same, it was a strange sort of defence to try and change the Gothic to Le Corbusier. There did not seem to be much point to the transforma-

49

tion, as the concrete shells would make larger targets for bombs and shells. Of course, there was always the possibility that they might be bomb-proof, but that did not seem to be likely, as it would have necessitated a weight which would have prevented their being lifted into place.

Anyhow, it was sheer tomfoolery to raise these bulwarks against one unarmed man. What damage could he do to even the fretted brick-work? He was friendly and they could not suspect him of hiding fleets of aeroplanes, or batteries of guns, in his jacket pockets. However, this display of the city's fortifications did one good thing: it showed him that the inhabitants, or their rulers, were as frightened by him as he was by them.

The balloon was hovering at a height of about ten feet above his head. "Ahoy there, ahoy there!" someone was calling. He was not, however, going to show that he had seen the balloon, and pointedly ignoring it, he kept on towards the city.

The ground upon which he was walking was unlike the firm springy turf of the previous evening; moorland, with bright green patches marking out the bogs, and sphagnum moss lying pink, and pale green, and a withered sandy colour, round the roots of the bog-myrtle and the heather.

A kestrel flew above him, swooping and stooping in the air every now and again as it saw a movement in the heather, recovering itself just before it fell like Icarus, noting the movement trivial, perhaps the jump of a grasshopper or the scurry of a vole entering its burrow.

Snipe zig-zagged noisily away, hares perked their long frightened ears as they paused on little mounds of peat, and a covey of grouse whirled away, their strong and supple wings beating the air with a noise like the pro-pellers of a squadron of aeroplanes. It seemed to be rare for the balloon to venture beyond the city boundaries for no sign of familiarity came from any animal.

CHAPTER FOUR

T HE accents of command had died from the voice of the man in the balloon, who was now using honeyed wheedling tones in the effort to make Christopher pay him some measure of attention.

"Please, dear man," he said, "please, look at me. We're so lonely up here. Won't you talk to us? Please, O please, be nice! We didn't mean to give you a fright, but we hadn't played with the whistle for such a long time, that we just had to let it give one really loud toot. Please, please, forgive us. We didn't really mean it."

" Sissies," Christopher muttered. "I'm damned if I'll accept their bloody crawling apologies. They're up to some game, and they won't get me off my guard with all their niceness."

He stepped on over the moor, avoiding the slushy places and skirting the bogs. He picked a handful of rushes, and began plaiting them into a long strip, just to show the aeronauts that he did not care about them, and that, if they wished, they could continue being nice to the empty air. He stripped the silky white pith out of the rushes before he plaited them, as he found that they broke, when bent, if the pith was left in. He put a piece of pith in his mouth and found it tasteless.

If it took him long enough to reach the city, he thought that he would almost have plaited a long enough strip to make a straw hat. He had never seen a green straw hat, but thought that one would mix well with the mad world in which he had landed.

51

The navigator had changed his tactics. The balloon itself was very low indeed, so that the gondola hung only a foot or two in front of Christopher's face, and the spokesman was leaning out of the stern, his hands outstretched in an attitude of prayer, so close that his fingers would have flicked Christopher's nose if he had not been careful to avoid such an intimacy.

"Please, dear darling man," he was saying, "don't be angry with us, please! We only let off the hooter in your honour, and we didn't mean to make you jump. Didn't you like our nice display of fireworks? They were all for you, to let you see how nice we think you are. You know, the way you're treating us is really a bit thick. We only meant to be nice, and we've apologized for any inconvenience we may have caused you, and we do so much want to be friends. We really *are* rather nice, you know, and you'll find *that* once we're better acquainted. Please, O please, do say something to show us you're not angry."

Christopher was finding it very difficult to ignore the balloon and the man leaning out at the stern. He could not look down, in case he bumped his head on the gondola and looking up he saw nothing but the shining aluminium body. He was irritated by this pestering, and had no wish to have a friendship thrust upon him.

He tried walking in a zig-zag, but the helmsman was very skilful, seeming to read Christopher's thoughts, and the balloon not so much followed his movements as seemed to anticipate them. He tried to walk faster, and once or twice managed to gain on the gondola, and ducked his head beneath it to try and pass, but the balloon dipped lower, bending him almost double.

The spokesman's entreaties for forgiveness were becoming more pressing, and he seemed to be trying to put his arms round Christopher's neck; presumably to give him a great big hug and a smacking kiss, to make things up.

Irritated, Christopher lifted his hand to strike away the importunate arms. His hand was grasped firmly, and the man said, "Ooo, you *really do* want to make friends, really and truly? I knew you wouldn't be angry with us for long. You *are* a nice man. Would you like a ride in our lovely balloon?"

Before Christopher had time to protest that they had misread his action, another man leaned over the stern and caught hold of him. The two of them raised him off the ground and, at the same moment, the balloon lifted high in the air, carrying him with it.

He could not struggle, for if the men released him he would fall hundreds of feet to be smashed on the peaty earth. When he got back to the city he would go to *Him* and explain that *His* men were insulting and that he wished to receive an apology and compensation for the way in which they had man-handled him.

If the men had grabbed him it was up to them to see that he was taken on board the balloon in safety, he certainly was not going to help them. They lowered a rope with a bowline in it, and swung the loop against his legs. He could have slipped through it and found a secure seat, but he continued to hang, a dead weight, while the crew bustled about trying to pull him in. The man who had hold of his arm tugged hard and managed to raise his forearm on to the sill.

He began treating it as a cross between a lever and a rope, nearly dislocating the elbow. It hurt so much that Christopher shouted, "Ow, for God's sake don't do that, you'll break my arm!"

"O dear man," his captor replied, "I'm so sorry, I didn't mean to hurt you, I was just trying to pull you to safety. It's really very dangerous to hang the way you're hanging, with no support but our arms. Please, O please, forgive me! I swear I didn't mean to hurt you. Shake hands to show there's no bad feeling, and that you understand."

He released his hold on the arm and stuck his hand out. Christopher swung in a wide arc, held only by the other man's grip on the collar of his jacket. As he swung, he saw the moor; it seemed to be miles below him. The man who had dropped his arm gave an agonized squeak, and threw out the bowline once more.

This time Christopher did not hesitate, but put his leg through the loop and grasped the rope with both hands. The hold on his collar was released suddenly, and the rope was paid out so that he found himself swinging through the air, about a hundred feet from the balloon, with only the thin cord between him and the plunge down on to the moor.

The crew of the balloon were a funny lot of jokers, to try and make friends with him, and then subject him to this sort of treatment. He looked up and saw several heads peering over the gondola. "Haul up," he shouted, "I can't hang on like this for ever. I may need to let go!"

Slowly, ever so slowly, the men on board started to pull him in and, as they did so, he spun like a top, so that he was near to letting go from sheer giddiness by the time he reached the firm metal sides of the gondola. He did not resist but let them heave him in. Then he fell on the floor and was violently sick.

Through a haze of nausea he noticed one of the men swabbing up the vomit with a cloth, just as fast as he spewed, and he heard the man who had held his arm speaking, in a gentle placatory voice, "There, there, old man! Do you feel sick? Poor old man, you'll be better in a minute. It won't last long."

Then he heard another voice, stern and rather abrupt, saying, "Drink this." He saw a glass in an outstretched hand and grasped it. The raw spirit made him gasp and

54

choke but, after a minute or so, his eyes cleared and he was able to look about him.

The gondola was practically empty. One of the crew was stowing away the rope in a neat locker. At the bow end a man sat on a seat holding a steering wheel, beside controls which resembled those of an ordinary motor-car.

Christopher looked to see who it was who had given him the glass of spirits (he could not name the drink as it was none that he had tasted previously), and saw the man in the leather suit, whom he had last seen seated on a high stool, tearing the petals from flowers.

He still held a large bunch of flowers in one hand, and, as Christopher glanced at him, he raised them to his nose and sniffed delicately. Christopher rose, finding his sickness had vanished. The deck of the gondola was surprisingly steady.

The man in the leather suit beckoned to him to follow, and led the way towards a hatch in the fabric of the balloon. One of the crew dodged between them to open the hatch, and a flight of steps slid down to the floor of the gondola; he bowed politely as he passed him.

They climbed for quite a distance, and then another hatch opened above their heads as the man in the leather suit twirled a combination-lock, set at the side of one of the rungs. They entered a large room with a thick glass roof.

His companion went across to a huge desk that nearly filled one end of the room, and sat down, while Christopher looked around curiously. One side of the room was lined with books, heavy calf-bound volumes with their titles inscribed in large gold letters on the spines, *The Proceedings of the Law and Zoological Society*. The idea of having one society to deal with these dissimilar activities was peculiar, but really no madder than many of the other oddities he had come across.

The walls were finished a dull bronze, and on one of them there was displayed a portrait of the man in the leather suit, twice as large as life. The original of this colossus rustled some papers on his desk and coughed, the brief official cough to attract attention. " Name, please?"

"My name is Christopher Aukland, Mr—er—er?"

The man wrote in a large book which Christopher observed, with some faint surprise, was identical with the volumes of *Proceedings*.

"I think you'd better call me Omar," he said slowly. "That is the name by which I am known to the people. Tell me how you came to our city, and what you intend to do now you are here."

Christopher gave him a rough outline of his adventures and finished by saying, "Now, if you please, I would very much like to send a telegram to my parents, as they will be worried about me. I would also be very glad if you could introduce me to my consul, so that I can borrow my fare home and arrange for a temporary passport. By the way, though I am grateful to you for your hospitality, I think you might have ordered your crew to treat me rather more gently. They pulled me about and forced me into your balloon without my consent. Also, I have only had some fruit to eat to-day and, consequently, am rather hungry."

Omar looked at Christopher closely as he took an aluminium tube from his pocket. "Hungry, eh?" he enquired, "take these and you'll be all right for a bit." He handed over two brown pills, veined with green, and continued, "I'm afraid that I cannot permit you to send a telegram at the present juncture, that is the prerogative of the official classes only. As for your consul here, well, I suppose I'd better tell you that we have no diplomatic relations with any foreign country. You will just have to be content until *He* decides what is to be done with you.

I have given instructions that you are to be received into the home of two of our ordinary citizens, W and Y, a male and a female, who will give you information about your behaviour. I trust that you will show no unseemly surprise when you see them, for, naturally, they are not as complete as you and I, but I'm sure you will find them very decent people, in spite of their deficiencies. You will, of course, be promoted when you have shown yourself capable of holding a position of responsibility. I am afraid that until then you cannot be permitted to hold any communication with any problematical outside world."

"But this is absurd," Christopher protested. "You can't do this to me. I am not a native of your country, and my Government will make the strongest representations to your government if you interfere with the liberties of one of their subjects. I have no desire, whatsoever, to become a petty official in your country. I arrived here by accident and demand my freedom now. If you are unwilling to help me, then, at least, you can land me outside the city boundaries and allow me to find my own way home. I hope you will do this at once."

Omar leaned forward, the corners of his mouth curled by the shadow of a smile.

"My dear Aukland," he said smoothly, "I am afraid that you do not realize your position. You may not have wished to enter our country, but by doing so unwittingly you have broken a great many laws. You crossed our frontier without permission, and without a passport or identification papers. The punishment for having no papers can be anything up to life imprisonment as a worker in the aluminium works—not, as a rule, a very long period. You are in no position to choose what you wish to do. I, acting in *His* name, tell you what you are to do, and you do that, quickly and well. I give the orders here and you obey them."

He paused to light a cigar which he took from a large cedar-wood humidor on the desk, and went on, "Now, if you are sensible, there is nothing to prevent your becoming an official of good standing. Then you can reconsider your wish to return to your own country. I am sure that you will find that your first thoughts were hasty, and you will prefer to remain with us."

Christopher, tired of standing, pulled a chair from a corner, and sat on it. "When I am talking to you, you stand," Omar barked. "I can see that you have a great deal to learn, and I will instruct Y and W accordingly."

"I am not your puppet yet," Christopher retorted, remaining seated. "I didn't ask to be brought into your filthy little airship, and I'm only here under protest. I do not wish to become a servant of your State, and I demand, as a free man, that you have me conducted to your frontier and there set at liberty. You need not fear that you will suffer by such an action, for my Government is notoriously generous to those States which co-operate in the care of its nationals. If you yourself cannot do this, I demand, as a free man employing his hereditary rights, to be taken before the head of your State that I may present my case, and demand to be set at liberty. I demand an interview with someone higher than a stuck-up jack-in-office."

"That," Omar was suave, "is impossible. No one can see *Him* but myself, *His* chief liaison officer. Also, my impetuous friend, I would warn you that, if you wish to be successful or comfortable here, you must not employ terms of abuse when speaking to your superiors. That will be all."

He gestured vaguely with one hand to show that the interview was at an end, pressing a bell set flush in the desk. Christopher did not consider that everything had been said which should have been, and started to speak, but before he had spoken more than a word or two he

58

noticed that two members of the crew were standing beside him.

They beckoned towards the hatch, and Christopher hesitated. They grabbed his elbows and ran him to the opening. One of them leaned over and shouted, "Ready there?" The answer was muffled but apparently satisfactory, for the men pulled Christopher over the hatch and, despite, his struggles, let him drop. The tunnel which had taken a minute or two to climb did not seem nearly so long. Christopher landed in a tarpaulin placed ready to catch him.

He was rolled out on the smooth aluminium deck, and the crew, without any concern for him, started rolling up the tarpaulin and stowed it away in a locker.

The man who was known to Christopher as the spokesman came forward. "Dear man," he said, "Omar's compliments to you, and will you please put on this suit. He says he can't have his prospective officials going round looking like collections of old clothes. It's not fair. He must like you more than he likes me. I do wish he'd let me have a leather suit."

Christopher took the clothes which were offered to him and found they were made of suede, and certainly looked as though they would be more comfortable than his old suit, which had suffered during his journey. He looked round the cabin to see where he could change, as he did not relish the idea of undressing before the interested eyes of the crew.

The spokesman said, "Come this way, dear." And led the way to a partition beside the driver. Christopher found himself in a small lavatory. He shut the door and locked it, to the audible disappointment of the crew.

He stowed his precious stones in various pockets of the suit, which fitted him well, and, rolling his old clothes in a bundle, left the lavatory.

Immediately one of the crew came forward and took

59

the bundle, to place it neatly in a locker. They had, Christopher thought, a mania for neatness on the balloon, for as soon as something had been used it was stowed away in one of the innumerable lockers. The man who had put away his clothes had apparently read Christopher's name on the collar of his jacket, for he returned and addressed him by name: "Christopher, would you like a cigarette?"

Christopher took one from the proffered packet, and the spokesman lit it for him, saying, "Christopher, ducky, you know it's not really too bad here, if Omar likes you, and I'm sure he does, for he's given you the leather suit I wanted. You'll soon get used to it. We're just going to have a cup of coffee. Will you join us?"

Christopher nodded, thinking that he had somehow got into a flying madhouse. A member of the crew opened one of the lockers and took out a thermos flask and several cups, and poured out coffee, sweetened to a syrup. The spokesman, who was called Dom, remarked, "We'll soon be home now, dears. You know, darlings, Chris does make me jealous. I thought I was a snip for the next leather suit. Chris, sweetheart, next time Omar talks to you, do be a duck and tell him you think it's about time I got a leather suit. Tell him how good I am, and I'm sure he'll listen to you, for really and truly he must like you an awful lot."

So far the driver had not moved from his hunched position and had not spoken. Now, as the balloon was slowly circling in its descent, he turned his head. Christopher nearly cried out, for the man had no face—merely eyes and holes for nostrils and mouth. Though he knew it was rude, Christopher could not help staring. He felt, however, that apart from being rude, his astonishment was probably unkind, for obviously the man must have met with some horrible accident.

Dom followed his eyes, saying, "O, I forgot, dear, you

60

haven't seen them yet. Rather thrilling, aren't they, and they're awful he-men, too. That's one of the citizens. They haven't got our looks you know. His name is Bec, and he's one of the best. I stay with him. Don't I, Bec, darling?"

The driver pursed the opening that did duty for a mouth into the obscene semblance of a kiss, and then turned back to his controls. Dom saw Christopher shudder, and put an arm round him, saying, "It's all right, dear. You'll just have to get used to their looks, for Omar says you're to live with two of them till you've settled down. They're really frightfully nice, but get a bit embarrassed if we, the officials, look at them as though they were unnatural. After all, they're just as real as you or I, and the only reason they feel shy is because some people look on them as oddities. I'll ask Omar if I can take you round to introduce you to Y and W, so's you won't feel so strange. You are a funny man, Chris."

He went to one of the lockers, taking out a hand-telephone into which he spoke. The thought of living with the faceless people occupied Christopher's mind to such an extent that he did not listen to Dom's conversation. When he had re-cradled the phone, Dom said, "That's all right now, my dear, the boss says I'm to look after you for a little, and to see that you don't get up to mischief. Come on now, ducks. We're aground."

Christopher had not felt the balloon come to rest, nor heard her engines stop, and realized, for the first time, that no noise had penetrated into the gondola.

The crew threw open a hatch in the middle of the deck, and started to file out. Christopher had hoped to see Omar again to make another protest about the summary treatment he was receiving, and to see whether he could buy his freedom with some of the precious stones he had found in the desert. However, Omar did not appear, and Dom answered Christopher's enquiries.

61

"O, the boss does not bother to land when we do, dearie. He comes and goes just as he pleases. He's a nice chap, and so lucky. Your luck is in, too, if he takes a fancy to you. He once took a fancy to me, so I know. He'll do all sorts of things for you, and you'll be an official before you know where you are."

They were in a building which looked like a church, though it had all the fittings of an aerodrome; squat black chaser planes, machine-guns nestling in their wings, stood beside helicopters, and the walls were hung with air-screws of all sorts and of all materials—aluminium, plastics, wood and stainless steel. However, the windows were not glazed with the usual wire-netting and glass, protection against fire, but with extraordinarily bad and garish stained glass. They showed men, some with the faces Christopher knew, and others faceless like the citizens, occupied in various activities connected with building, making bricks, erecting walls and carving gargoyles.

Dom led Christopher between the rows of aeroplanes and out into the street. The houses were of all sorts and sizes, and seemed to vie with one another in the elaborateness of their decorations. There were plaques on some, stating absurdities (the fact that so-and-so had *never* lived in the house), and others were stuck all over with sea-shells—clams, oysters, dog-whelks and the rest, while others again were ornamented with bottles of all sorts, from the little green ones crying 'Poison' to the huge ones which stand, filled with coloured waters, in chemists' windows, all carefully set in cement to form a pattern or spell out a name.

They went about three hundred yards without meeting anyone except officials, and then Christopher came face to face with three of the featureless women. They resembled the pictures of Humpty Dumpty which he had drawn on egg-shells when a child, except that then he had made some attempt to show a nose and a fullness of the lips that was completely absent in these faces.

He considered that his treatment was harsh, for he was virtually a prisoner, or even a kindergarten child, being told to do this or that, and to study the rules of correct behaviour.

Unfortunately, escape seemed to be no easy matter; one of these squat fighters would catch him up before he had time to travel far—if there was a *normal distance* in this place, for *He* seemed to have some power over space, making it expand or contract according to *His* wishes.

It was all very muddling, and he hoped that some way of escape from Omar would present itself. By this time, he was sure, his parents would almost have ceased worrying about him, and would have given him up for lost. His father would be wearing a broad black band on his left arm when he went to the office, and both his parents would invest the vanished Christopher with almost mythical qualities, referring to "our dear boy," saying how good he had always been at school, and such a help about the house.

His father, who was always grumbling about municipal affairs, had probably taken out a writ against the town council, and, if so, Christopher wondered at what high price a judge and jury would value his absent body. He thought of the high praise he would receive from his father's counsel, and then of the row there would be when he turned up at home. It would take one or two jewels to placate his father, but it would be worth the whole boiling of them to be home again.

All this time Dom had been leading him round corners and neither of them had spoken at all. They entered an avenue of the most absurd-looking villas, and walked down towards the end of it. Dom opened the elaborate wrought iron gate of the last house, and they walked up

63

a path made from the crown-corks of beer bottles, set side by side to hide the cement beneath, towards a porch made from the jaw-bones of a whale. Dom leaned forward to knock at the door, which was covered completely by a shockingly bad painting of one of the featureless women.

"W," he remarked briefly, as he tapped twice on the place where there should have been a nose.

CHAPTER FIVE

CHRISTOPHER braced himself to meet the faceless woman as he heard steps approaching the inside of the door. However, it was not opened by W, but by a young woman with perfectly normal features. "I'm afraid W's out," she began, and then recognized Dom. "O, it's you, Dom, is it? And this is Christopher? We got a message about him from the radio station."

She looked closely at Christopher and he felt that she was counting the stubble on his unshaved face. Then she said, "I'm Mali, and I live here. You know, they board us out all over the place. I see you're a lucky one, and Omar's taken a fancy to you. He rarely takes a notion for one of us girls. Come in now."

Dom kissed Christopher full on the mouth and spoke, " Good-bye, ducks. I'm hoping that you'll be around a lot. Remember and put in a good word for me next time you see the boss."

The hall of the house had, apparently, at some time been papered with white paper, but since then the occupants of the house had decorated it with transfers of all sorts—butterflies, fishes, tropical flowers, sea-shells and the adventures of comic animals. Mali led him upstairs; the banisters were elaborate fretwork, enamelled all colours.

He was taken into a small room, and, for a moment, he thought that something had gone wrong with his eyesight, for the table looked like a chandelier and the light like a table, the former being made of cut-glass, with excrescences sticking out all over the place, and the latter, it would seem, of mahogany. In a corner was a box-bed, but a box-bed unlike any that Christopher had ever seen, for the posts were carved into perpendicular Gothic spires, with small stained glass windows painted on them. The rest of the room appeared to be almost entirely occupied by the most useless collection of ornaments imaginable; pottery dogs jostled china cats covered with roses, bamboo tables were swamped by cloths with long silky tassels, glass fish swam over mirrors, calendars dating years back hid one wall, and pressed flowers were gummed all over another.

Mali said, "This is your room, Christopher. W and Y will be back soon, and will give you a meal. Would you like me to show you round the house?"

Christopher said he would like to see the house, thinking that he might as well do that as anything else, and followed her down the corridors with their arched roofs and elaborate carpets. He wanted to ask her what he should say to Y and W when they turned up, but felt that it would probably appear a stupid question. However, she must have sensed his uneasiness, for she said, "What's worrying you? Not sure how to take the citizens? Don't you worry. All you have to do is to treat them like ordinary people, and they'll be all right. What's the time now?"

She looked at a clock, set in a golden sun, and continued, "Five o'clock. Well, they should be back before long, and then they'll give us our supper. You know it's lights-out at a quarter to eight when the bulwarks go up. Even the officials, except the big shots, have to go to bed then, unless they've got special passes from Omar. You'll find it pays to stick in with him, for he's *His* lieutenant, and gives all the orders, and, if he likes you, you will receive special privileges and be quickly promoted to the first grade. I, for instance, am a first-grade woman."

Christopher was about to ask for details of this grading system when he heard the front door open. Mali led him down to the hall to greet a man and woman who were standing there. They split their slit mouths in an expression which, Christopher guessed, was intended to convey pleasure. For a moment he wondered how the faceless citizens were distinguished from one another; then, as they moved into a better-lighted room off the hall, he noticed that their initials, Y and W, were impressed upon their foreheads, the bland skin puckered by the brand.

"How do you do, Mr. Christopher?" Y said. "I hope you will enjoy your stay with us. I know we may seem strange at first, for I have been informed that you have not previously encountered citizens of our flawless visage. I expect you will soon, however, learn to appreciate our normality. My wife will serve supper in a minute. To-morrow, if you like, I will take you out when we go, and will show you the city. I have been granted special leave for this purpose, as Mr. Omar wishes you to become a fully-fledged official with the least possible delay."

There was something mechanical about Y's voice, reminding Christopher of a gramophone, and making him feel that each word had been rehearsed; however, the tone was pleasant and, so long as he did not stare at the blank face, Christopher found that he could almost imagine himself home again, listening to the exposition of the press and radio by his father's friends, "those who when the saving thought came shot it as a spy."

The dining-room, where they now stood, was a more fantastic version of his bedroom, with more elaborate ornaments and a throng of palms, ferns, aspidistras and juniper bushes, each occupying a column of variegated marble.

W removed some plates from a cupboard disguised as a bookshelf with the glued-on backs of books, and, going to a hatch papered with a chromolithograph of a building like the Crystal Palace, brought out a steaming tureen. Settling on the assorted chairs (the one Christopher sat upon was made from the antlers of several stags) they started supper. While they ate no one spoke, and Christopher had the feeling that the gramophone could not run while it was being oiled.

Finally, Y produced a large box of cigarettes, decorated with Moorish arabesques and crescent moons, and handed it to Christopher. "Mr. Omar," he remarked, "sent these for you. They may help you towards a better understanding of his intentions, which are that you should be made as comfortable as possible."

They sat on in the room until it became dusk and the house was penetrated by a shrill whistle. "First hooter," Y said. "You'd better get up to your room and into bed. No lights in summer, so we need to hurry, as it's very dark after the bulwarks rise. Mr. Omar, however, gave me this torch for you—said you were a stranger to be treated kindly, sent messages for a good night's rest, and wishes for your health."

Carrying the square torch he was given, Christopher went up to his room and undressed slowly, hanging his clothes on crystal excrescences that stuck out from the mantel shelf. He had no night clothes, and, in the warm

67

weather, saw no need of them. The sheets were delight-fully cool after his previous night's sleep in his suit, and soon he started to doze.

He had just fallen asleep when the hooter sounded again, and the windows were blotted out by the rising of the concrete walls. Immediately after he heard the door of his room opening.

In the thin beam of his torch he saw Mali standing there smiling. "Are you all right?" she asked. "I thought you'd like to get settled in before I came up."

Christopher was startled; he had not expected that Omar's ideas of helping him to settle down would run to the extent of providing him with a woman. There must be a trap somewhere, and he would need to be careful. "Where do you sleep, Mali?" he asked, making his voice as negligent as possible.

"Here, you silly!" she replied. "Where did you think I'd sleep? I told you I was a first-grade woman official."

Christopher hesitated for a moment, and then said, "Oh! Do you often have to do this? Pretty poor job, isn't it?"

"It's my job," she replied, "and it's not at all a bad one—there are a lot of women who'd like to have it. It's not as though I was a second-grader and had to sleep with the citizens. I'm a first-grader, and can more or less choose whom I want. Anyhow, you don't seem to be very pleased with the idea? You're not one of *those*—you know—like the airmen?"

Christopher denied the imputation with vigour, and Mali seemed to be relieved. He thought it was undoubt-edly a strange town where they supplied their visitors with bed-mates; but it was too late, if he had wished to do so, to protest, for Mali obviously had nowhere else to sleep and was already nearly undressed.

She slipped into bed beside him, putting her arms round him, and said, "I'm not so bad really, am I? You were only a bit upset by its strangeness. Turn off your torch."

He put his arms round her and she started kissing him.

Waking after midnight, listening to Mali's breathing and trying to penetrate the darkness, heavy as a blanket, Christopher wondered what his father would say were he to see him now. His thoughts, as always, turned towards his return home. Escape, it seemed, would be difficult, but all obstacles would need to be surmounted. Horror struck him with the notion that he might have left the desert on the *wrong* side. If he had gone in the opposite direction, perhaps, he would have been safely home by this time.

He tossed restlessly in the bed. Mali turned towards him, mumbling, "What is it, dear?" She held him in her arms until he ceased to fret about an uncertain future.

When he woke Christopher found that the outer walls had already been lowered. The sun was streaming through the little gap between the lace curtains, tiny specks floating and dancing in the bright beam. He pulled himself up in the bed and looked down at Mali.

She still slept, all her hair scattered on the pillow round her face. He bent down to kiss her, but she woke and pushed him gently away. "No, no, my dear," she said, "you mustn't. Not in the mornings. *He* has forbidden it, saying it lowers efficiency throughout the ensuing day."

Christopher restrained his desire and the impulse to be rude about *His* interference with private matters. They dressed quickly and joined Y and W in the dining-room.

Expecting a green veined pill, Christopher was relieved to find a large plate of bacon and a steaming cup of coffee set before him. When he had finished, Y took up his bowler hat and Christopher noticed that the band was

69

pale violet, with his initial embroidered upon it, so that he could be identified even when his forehead was hidden.

The faceless creatures were not so terrifying in the morning light. He must be getting used to them, and, after all, it was not the poor devils' fault that they had neither noses nor ears nor lips, and that their eyes were set flush with their cheeks. He turned to Mali, asking, "Are you coming with us, to see that I find my way about all right?"

"No," she replied, "I've got to go to work this morning. But I'll see you again to-night, for I've been allotted to your case for a period of undetermined length."

Christopher wondered what work she did during the day, but decided that the question could wait for a more propitious moment. She must lead a pretty hard life though, having to work both night and day, even if her two activities were of different kinds, and he did not know whether they were.

Y carried a thin metal walking-stick, painted sky-blue, and gave Christopher another, exactly the same. "These are our passports," he said, "to show that we have been excused work for the day. This means that the city guardians will not trouble us. You must remember to carry yours when you go out, particularly if you are with anyone. I drew these from ordnance yesterday afternoon."

They walked along the fantastic streets, between the clotted swirls of the baroque and the lichenous encrustation of Gothic. Y asked Christopher where he would like to go first. He replied that there was only one place he knew, the place of the bleeding statues, and he would like to see them by daylight. Y spoke of these statues as though they were miracles, so Christopher refrained from questioning him about the tall gaunt pigeon-slayer as, by mentioning him, he might, firstly, hurt Y's feelings and,

70

secondly, be breaking the law, that law which he could not fathom.

There was an almost religious feeling about the square, and heavy curls of scented smoke rose from elaborate censers distributed on the tessellated pavement; these were tended by small boys with golden bellows. Beneath each statue a small group stood, each person gazing at the blood as if hoping that some prayer might be granted by virtue of the action of looking. All the statues represented some person or thing—judges, flowers, cats, airmen, angels and so forth—but one, which seemed to be merely a common block of stone.

This cube bled from a hole, about eighteen inches from the top, and was surrounded by a large crowd. These people dipped their fingers in the blood and smeared red scars across their foreheads. Christopher noticed that while the groups before the other statues were composed solely of the blank-faced citizens, round this block they were mingled with officials, vying with one another in the ardour with which they gazed upon it, and the avidity with which they scooped up the drops of blood.

Christopher asked Y the reason for this, and was told that this was a statue of *Him*. "The officials, as you will understand, Mr. Christopher, are not so much in need of help as we common citizens, and consequently are forbidden to make requests to the other statues. But as that is a statue of *Him*—representing *Him* bleeding for *His* people, all men and women are aided by the blood. It is still a square block of stone, as it will not become a statue until *He* dies, when it will, miraculously, assume *His* shape and the people will know *Him*. That, of course, will never happen, as *He* is immortal, and beyond the reach of death."

Anxious to know more about this mysterious figure who was never seen, and who ruled by proxy of Omar, Christopher started plying Y with questions.

71

"We do not know *Him*, and it is generally thought that *He* converses only with Mr. Omar. There may be one or two others with whom *He* is familiar, but they have nothing to do with us. As for *Himself*, we have not the slightest idea who *He* is. Some say that *He* is in the habit of coming among *His* people in disguise, but I, personally, think that unlikely. Every now and then rumours fly round the city that *He* proposes to display *Himself*, but these are always denied officially.

A few years back there was serious trouble, for a renegade official started a movement among those who wished to see their rulers. The main plank in his platform, his name was Mogor, was that *He* was dead and had been so for years. Like all hot heads, Mogor had little difficulty in gathering a crowd of irresponsibles to support him, and they marched through the city to demand of Mr. Omar that *His* body should be produced. Naturally, the army soon suppressed the rising, and Mogor was executed. It was after this insurrection that the statues began to bleed."

Wondering at the gullibility of the people, Christopher asked Y where the blood came from.

"That is a question which must not be asked," Y straightened himself up, and spoke in a horror-struck whisper, "It is illegal, *He* has forbidden it. If the guardians had heard you, it would have meant your immediate arrest, in spite of your being a stranger here. You must be careful in what you say—for my sake as well as for your own. If you are arrested I am at once executed for not giving you better instruction in deportment. Come on, now. We will leave this dangerous place."

CHAPTER SIX

T HEY wandered through the streets, but did not enter any of the buildings which Y pointed out as museums and picture galleries. Christopher would not be admitted until he had received his ticket as a third-grade official, which, in addition to allowing him into these places, would automatically make him a member of The Officials Club. Naturally, Y assured him, the ordinary citizens were not permitted to enter the galleries under any circumstances, with the exception of the lowest rank of females, who were cleaners and whose work had to be finished before the arrival of the first official.

They returned to the villa for lunch, and after, Christopher told Y that he would like to rest in the house during the afternoon. Mali was not in to lunch, which W again prepared by opening a hatch and taking it out. Christopher questioned her about these hatches.

"Well," she said, "you see, I don't do any cooking. The government decided, long before my time, that it would be more economical to provide the citizens with all meals, deducting a small sum from their salaries in return for the convenience. This means that I can work without the perpetual worry of home things. The meals are delivered at the hatch by a system of vacuum tubes. This, as you can see, does away with all the old-fashioned fatigue, and I can work longer without requiring a rest. However, I can get a holiday if I am picked to have a baby. *He* is really very thoughtful about things like that, and grants us leave for nine months, from the end of the first three months."

73

Once Y and W had left the house, Christopher wondered whether he had not a chance to send a message home, and went into the small room off the dining-room. He picked up the receiver and a voice spoke, "Number, please?"

"I would like a telegram, please. This is WY4937 calling."

"Hold on a minute, number WY4937, while I connect you. Your name, please? Yes, I must have your name before I connect you. Aukland? Thank you, Mr. Christopher."

Hell, he thought, it's going a bit far when the girls in the telephone-exchange know me by my first name. There was obviously something cunning about the phone. It was a trap of some sort. The voice spoke again, "I am afraid that the line is occupied at the moment. Can I ring you back at WY4937? Thank you."

Christopher replaced the receiver and sat down in an armchair, fiddling with a large amethyst crystal. He was sure that he would get into trouble over this effort, as Omar had told him that only officials could send telegrams. But, in spite of that, there was always the chance that the wire might get through. Then his Government would protest about this enforced detention of one of their subjects, and Christopher would be escorted to the frontier and put on a train for home.

If not, say the wire failed, well, he could not be very much worse off than he was at present, virtually a prisoner in this queer city.

They were taking a long time about connecting him with the telegram department. Perhaps the operator had informed the city guardians and, even now, they were on their way to arrest him.

The telephone rang, and he returned to the bamboo table and picked up the receiver. "Hullo," he said, "is that telegrams?"

A voice answered him, "Telegrams, Mr. Christopher. Just a moment while I connect you with the sending operator."

Wires jangled and bells rang. It was a man's voice that resumed. "Go ahead now," he said, "I am ready."

Disregarding the proportions of Y's telephone bill, Christopher made no efforts to cut down the number of words in his telegram, but dictated one long enough to satisfy the curiosity and to pacify the worries of his parents. When he had finished, he paused and said, "Got all that?"

The man's voice replied, and there was a menacing sound from the very-first word. "Yes, thank you, I have got everything. This, my dear Christopher, is Omar. I thought I told you that you were not to attempt to telegraph until you had a permit from me? Do you not remember, my dear Christopher? This little matter of disobedience may have to be dealt with severely. I want you to hold yourself in readiness to receive my orders. The telegram you have just dictated will not, of course, be transmitted. It will be filed in your folder."

"Who the hell do you think you are to give me orders?" Christopher shouted into the microphone. "I am a free agent, and will do exactly as I like, without any interference from you. For my own actions I am answerable to one person—myself!"

"Not here," the rejoinder was gentle, "and please, my dear Christopher, have some respect for my ear-drums and do not bellow into the telephone. It is childish, and also happens to be forbidden by law. Didn't you read the instructions on the phone before you used it. I am afraid, Christopher, that you have a great deal to learn, and the first thing you must appreciate is that my orders are given *to be obeyed*. I am *His* agent, and consequently have absolute power over you. You will kindly do *exactly* as you are told in future. I will not stand for more trouble from you. Your pride and your presumptuous behaviour may have been slightly amusing to begin with, but they are fast becoming boring."

Omar seemed to be about to continue, but Christopher seized the receiver with both hands and ripped it from its fittings. At least, he thought, I've silenced him for a while. He may have power over me, but I'm damned if I'm going to listen to his sneers. I'm not his chattel, and I won't obey him unless it suits me."

Suddenly Omar's voice continued, "That, my impetuous young friend was a very rash action. You should not do things like that, or you'll find yourself in trouble. It's all right, you cannot smash the speaker which I am now using."

Christopher had started round the room, to tear down the carving and the printed drapery in his search for the loud-speaker. Frustrated, he threw himself angrily in an armchair, while Omar resumed.

"Can't you see, you young fool," his voice was kindly and heavily avuncular, "that I'm doing my best for you. You should be glad indeed that I am so disposed towards you, otherwise you would, by this time, have been arrested or even executed. Please do not try me any further, for, though I personally am a merciful man, *He*, from his higher altitude, cannot be expected to see frailness as I see it. From *His* point of view, you are merely a nuisance, a fragment of grit in the smoothly-oiled cogs, and as such it is only logical that you should be eliminated. Naturally, you will have to be punished for your disobedience to me personally—that is necessary for the sake of discipline —but I will make that punishment as light as possible. I think that you should make a good official once you have settled down. Good-bye for the present. Remember what I have told you."

Christopher sat looking at the mess he had made, feeling rather ashamed of himself, for, after all, neither

Y nor W had been responsible for his humiliation, and it was their house he had been smashing. He managed to put the telephone together by twisting the wires, and asked the operator whether it was all right. She replied that it would require to be inspected by a linesman.

He started to clear up the room, hiding the evidence of his lost temper. As he was doing this he heard the front door open, and redoubled his efforts to remove its curiously debauched appearance. Mali entered.

"I hear you've been in trouble," she said, "and that the boss isn't too pleased with you. You really mustn't do things like this, as it gives a lot of unnecessary work to the already overburdened officials. Even if you can't believe that Omar has absolute power over you, my dear, I think it would be much better if you, at least, made some pretence of believing, and tried to carry out any orders you received. Believe me, my sweet, obedience here is the only way to get on."

She had barely finished speaking before there was a knock at the front door. Mali went and opened it, returning with a man whom she announced as the telephone inspector, a short, fussy little man who fiddled with the wires till he gave himself an electric shock. Then he rang up the exchange and spoke querulously.

"Someone here's been making a mess of the receiver. Please tell the director of workmen I would like to see him at once. Tut, I gave myself a nasty shock, a very nasty shock, and this is an urgent case."

As he rang off he turned to Christopher, "You're very lucky, young man. You can get into serious trouble for damaging the city communications. If Omar had not intervened on your behalf, let me tell you, the corporation would have sued you for wilful destruction, and you'd have been fortunate, very fortunate, to have got off with less than a life sentence."

Under the pretence of inspecting the rest of the room,

the inspector tried to hear what Mali and Christopher were saying to one another. They became silent and remained so until someone else came to the door. This was the director of workmen, and he, too, fussed around the telephone, driving the hair-thin wires under his nails until convinced that a workman was necessary.

Going to the window he shouted at a citizen who was passing. "Hey, you, can you mend telephones?" The faceless man came in and had the phone repaired in a matter of minutes, while the two officials looked on and praised the neatness of his handiwork.

Christopher did not think there was a great deal to praise, as he could have done the job himself, given the tools; however, since it seemed to be the thing to do, he also applauded. At once they turned on him and, in unison, squashed him, snapping, "Don't do that. You made this mess."

The citizen left the house, and the officials shook hands, congratulating one another on their handling of a difficult situation. The inspector turned to Christopher, saying, "If anything like this happens again you won't get off so easily. I've been promised the next prosecution, and you were a serious case." The director of workmen remarked, "You've upset my whole afternoon by your tantrums. I am displeased with you."

Christopher was about to reply, to their retreating backs, that he did not care if they were displeased, but Mali covered his mouth with hers and pulled him down.

Lying in bed beside Mali that night, Christopher made up his mind that he would attempt to sell some of his jewels next day, and bribe his way out of the country with the proceeds. He decided against telling Mali of his intentions, as he did not know what kind of work she did during the day—she might be a female city guardian for all he knew—and because he remembered that she had known about his adventures with the telephone, before she had entered the house.

He heard her breathing quicken and knew that she was awake. "What is it dear?" she asked. "What's worrying you?"

"Nothing," he lied. "I was just wondering what other difficulties I would encounter in this strange town of yours. I don't like the idea of being ordered about, but I suppose I may grow used to it."

"There you are, sweet," she said, "I knew you would realize that soon. You know I like you more than any of the other men I've had. If you like I can get my assignment to your case lengthened. I know that Omar would consent, because it would show that you were settling down. Then, once you became a proper official, and were promoted, we could get married if you liked the idea. It is really much more pleasant here once you are married. You receive all sorts of benefits, and they can't send a wife out on an unpleasant assignment, as they can send me at present."

Feeling rather a swine for his deception, Christopher started kissing her instead of replying. She held him tightly and seemed to be happy, which made him feel worse than ever.

"I say, Mali," he began hesitantly, "about us getting married. Will you mind leaving here when I get my permit to return to my own country?"

She was silent for a minute or two. "*If* you get away," she said, "I will come with you. But I must tell you, my dear, that I don't think it likely that you will be allowed to leave. Even if Omar wanted to let you go, I feel certain that *He* would veto the idea, for people never leave the city—at least, I can't remember anyone leaving all the time I've been an official."

"What do you do during the day, Mali? I don't suppose this job of looking after people is a full-time one, is it?"

"No," she replied, "I work in the identification bureau, seeing that people's cards are up to date, and so on. I expect I'll have to fill in your one in a day or so, making you a student-official of this city. You know that officially, and everything here must be done officially, you have no status in this town till you have a card, and till then you are almost non-existent in the eyes of the officials. I'll try and hurry your card through as it's rather awkward to be without one."

As he dozed off to sleep again, Christopher realized that he was still a free man in the eyes of the law, and that he would need to leave very quickly, before the process of forcible naturalization was completed. He could not ask Mali to delay the production of his card without exciting her suspicions. He would make all his plans in the morning.

Wandering among the tortuous back streets, looking for a pawnbroker's sign or a jeweller's shop, he noticed for the first time that no trains ran from this city; there were no fringed lines denoting railways on the maps that hung in prominent places. These maps, also, showed the daytime city in considerable detail, but gave no indication of the divisions provided by the concrete walls after sundown.

He looked in the Citizens' Library for relics of attempted flights, but found no signs of them among the reminders of notable crimes; nor did the history-books, concerned mostly with *His* rule, make any mention of escape. The city seemed to be rather like an egg, and Christopher wondered whether his escape would smash it like the emergence of a chick, pecking its way through the tissue which lined the chalky shell. Perhaps even the whole town would cease to exist once he left it, and would become one with the ruined city of the desert.

The whole affair at times took on the appearance of a dream. The horrors were the sort of horrors of which one dreamed, not the casual beastliness of the waking world. He felt that he himself was sane, but was forced to doubt the reality of the things about him, the creations of a disordered mind, the phantasies of a pipe-dream. These egg-faced citizens could have no reality.

The trouble here lay in the semblance of reality behind all the illusions; thus the bleeding statues were fed privately by the pigeon-man. He realized, also, that although W had spoken of babies, he had not encountered one of the smooth faces under the age of twenty, so that, perhaps, the featureless effect was the results of skilled plastic surgery.

He was behaving very badly to Mali, but that could not be helped. He had not asked to be supplied with a woman, and if accidents like that of falling in love occurred, they were not his fault. He told himself that he liked her, but that he liked the idea of his freedom better. He could not say what he meant by freedom, for he realized that, in truth, he had not been freer at home than he was in this queer city, but there the hedging rules had been less obvious, or had affected him, personally, less than they did here. At home he had been one person in a crowd, while here he stood out as a stranger among the natives, though hardly the one Christian in darkest Africa.

He admired the ingenuity displayed in the decoration of some of the villas, plastered as they were with all that was useless. There was one which had been covered with tiny squares of multi-coloured cloth until it resembled his grandmother's patchwork quilt, while another had been besprinkled, God alone knew how laboriously, with beads and little bits of broken glass, none larger than the nail of his little finger, sparkling like a kaleidoscope in the sun.

However, in all his wanderings, he saw no building operations in progress. The whole place seemed to have

81

been built and decorated straight off, and expansion, save in decoration, forbidden since the date of completion.

Suddenly, on going back into the square, he noticed, on the far side, a shop which had previously escaped his notice. The window resembled a firework display. There indeed, was the jeweller's shop for which he sought. He went towards it, wondering how it had escaped his usually observant eyes.

As he passed *His* block of stone, masquerading as a statue of the unknown ruler, he dipped his finger into the bowl of blood and shook the glutenous drops off, muttering, "I hope there's some luck or virtue in you. I'm afraid, though, that you're a fraud and I must trust only in myself. I wonder what you are really like, and if the man who led the rising—(what was his name? Mogor, that's it)—was not right in thinking you dead for years. Anyhow, here's good luck to myself and a long nose to your stupid laws."

Excited by his luck, he stood before the jeweller's shop, fingering the larger stones in his pockets, his eyes dazzled by the brightness of the cut gems inside, in heavy settings designed to show off their richness. If the shop was not the only one, it was certainly one of the best in town, for the jewels were arranged in crowns and tiaras, as would suit a ruler and his closed circle. None of these trinkets was priced, but Christopher remembered that the better class jewellers at home had arranged their jewels in a similar manner, on black velvet, carefully wrinkled to give the effect of negligence and of disorder, to set against the precision of the facets that exposed the unimagined depths of the precious stones.

He looked round him and saw, to his horror, two of the city guardians eyeing him with apparent suspicion. However, he would have to make the best of it, pretending that he was an official with serious business to transact.

82

He turned and gazed at the guardians, meeting their eyes with a bold stare, and then walked up three steps into the moist dark interior of the shop.

There was no one there, and, though his opening of the door had rung a bell, no one appeared. For a minute he sat on a chair, upholstered in old gold plush, and then, rising, returned to the door. He saw that the city guardians had turned away from the shop and were strolling towards the other side of the square.

He opened the door so as to jangle the bell once more, and went back to his chair.

CHAPTER SEVEN

SUDDENLY, from the gloom behind the counter, a voice spoke. "Yes," it enquired peevishly, "what do you want?"

Christopher jumped to his feet and advanced towards the glass covered counter, which acted as an additional show-case. Behind it there stood a very small man, dressed in a uniform which made him seem like a replica or caricature of Napoleon Bonaparte.

"I say," he began with diffidence, "do you buy jewels?"

The little man laid a white slug of a hand on the counter and replied, "Yes—on occasions. Why? Have you got anything to show me? Think carefully before you answer."

Not knowing what he was required to think about, Christopher laid down three jewels, two blue diamonds and an emerald. The jeweller poked his neckless head forward. "Quite nice," he said, "so far as I can tell from

83

a casual glance. I will need to get my glass. Where, if it is not impertinent, my young sir, did you get them?"

"Before I came here I got caught in the desert and picked these up in my wanderings. How much are they worth?" Christopher blurted, and then felt unwise for showing such eagerness.

"There's no hurry, young man," was the reply. "So you got them in the desert, did you, huh? Well, I'll go and get my glass, and then, perhaps, I'll be able to give you some idea of their value. You young men are always in too much of a hurry. You've no ideas of dignity. Why, when I was a young man it often used to take us several days preliminary discussion before we so much as mentioned the deal we hoped to put through. But then, I suppose, times change. Sit down and wait till I come back, and don't go fussing around the door, ringing that beastly bell. Nearly deafened me, you did."

He moved slowly towards the back of the shop, and as he did so Christopher saw the reason of his smallness. He had no legs, and was moving on thick stumps thrust into a pair of dirty crimson carpet slippers.

Waiting for his return with the glass, Christopher was congratulating himself on the ease with which he was selling his stones, until he noticed, on a corner of the counter, a short black tube of the kind that watchmakers use, screwed into one eye, to examine the position of a balance wheel or the break in a hair-spring.

He rose to his feet and advanced towards the counter, to pick up his jewels and leave before the miniature Boney returned. He heard the door-bell jangle and saw the two city guardians who had been watching him.

He straightened up and turned to face them, telling himself that, after all, there was nothing criminal in a man trying to sell his own property. All the same, there was a horrible bulge in his throat, like a lump from badly-cooked porridge, and his stomach was heaving in time with his heavy heart.

He tried to look at the guardians nonchalantly, as if he was a customer whose business had been interrupted by the inopportune entrance of other customers. He hoped that they might be about some official business, and not inclined to interfere with him.

However, they approached him, saluting smartly. One of them addressed him, "Christopher? That's you, is it?"

"Yes. What is it?" Christopher bowed.

"We have come to ask you some questions, but before we do that, here is your identity card."

The spokesman held out a neat blue-bound booklet. Embossed on the buckram cover, in gold letters, was the legend, 'CHRISTOPHER aukland. Number:—Zp/qR 543 rTj.' Christopher held it in his hand for a moment, and then slid it into the pocket of his jacket, wondering what would come next. The guardians were closing in on him.

"Christopher. Acting under *His* orders, conveyed to me under the seal of Omar, I arrest you, for planning to leave the city without receiving *His* permission."

Christopher felt on the counter for a heavy ebony ruler he had noticed. Holding it behind his back, he swept his jewels into his pocket and, pulling himself upright, hit the speaker above the eyes.

The guardian went down as if he had been felled by a captive-bolt. Christopher turned towards the other man, who had grasped him by the arm. He got him down on the floor and was beating his head on the jade marble when he heard the slow tolling of a bell. This was the same bell that had warned the night watchman when he saw the pigeon-killer. Other guardians seemed to fill the shop to overflowing, and his arms were held so that he could not rise.

Pinned down, he saw them throw water on the stunned guardian, who sat up slowly, with the precision of a mechanical doll. "What happened?" he demanded, and then, catching sight of Christopher, he advanced menacingly towards him. "That is something more for which you will pay," he hissed, the villain in a melodrama. " Omar deals severely with those who dare assault the city guardians."

He slapped Christopher across the mouth, and at the sight of the salt blood dribbling, started to laugh immoderately. His laughter was infectious, and spread to the other guardians, who began to roll helplessly around the shop. Christopher felt the grip on his arms loosen as the paroxysms of laughter shook his captors. He managed to shake them off, and leaped on to the counter, smashing the glass top as he did so.

He would break free again, he thought, as he hit one of the suddenly sobered guardians on the nose and felt it crumple under the impact. Then his legs were grasped from the darkness, so strongly that he could do nothing, and he was swung round and deposited on the floor.

His captor was the small jeweller, who was now grinning up at his efforts to escape. He tried to smash the gaping grin from the aged face, but could not balance for a blow. Then he was held firmly on the floor by half a dozen guardians. None of them was laughing now.

Other guardians were congratulating the jeweller, patting him on the back, telling him he was a fine fellow. He shuffled slowly across to Christopher lying on the floor, his red clad feet moving like flayed slugs. He looked down from his small height and spat.

"Thought you could beat me, did you, eh?" he sneered. "Well, better men than you have thought that, and have found they couldn't beat old Crop—in spite of his lack of legs."

He took one of his stumps from its slipper and, leaning against the counter, waved it above Christopher's face, so that the puckered browny-red skin was just above his nose, and he could smell the hot sweat it distilled. He shut his eyes, hoping to escape from it, but felt its hard pressure on his mouth, and found he could not shut off the senses of feeling and hearing as he wished.

"Kiss, damn you, kiss it!" the jeweller snarled. "It's a better foot, and belongs to a better man than your feet do, though they be smooth as silk and sweet as milk. Kiss it, damn you!"

The picture of the obscene stump seemed to be cast by some magic-lantern on Christopher's eyelids, and he would have lifted them but they seemed glued shut. He shuddered violently, and could not restrain the flood of sickness that rose in his mouth and splattered on the stump.

He opened his eyes as one of the guardians pulled him upright. They were wiping him clean while others were trying to restrain the jeweller, who was frothing at the mouth, literally bubbling out large puffs of froth. Suddenly he found his voice and burst into a stream of blasphemy and obscenity, tracing Christopher's descent from every vile beast, by way of the most depraved vices.

The guardians started to hustle Christopher out of the shop, looking as though they were frightened of Crop and his violence, and unsure how long their companions could hold him away from Christopher.

Once outside the shop the guardians ceased to hold Christopher, and he walked with them like a man strolling with his friends, noticing, however, that they had arranged themselves in such a way that, if he had attempted to fly, any one of them would have caught him easily.

Brought down by number six shot like a snipe on a misty day on the moors, or like a wing three-quarter who, sprinting for the line, is tackled by the back.

Failure in his attempt was little, it meant no worse than previous captivity, but death was still the undesired solution. Proof, however, lacking, they could not convict him of intent to leave the Gothic and the concrete city.

Now, walking roads of opaque glass, they went towards an unknown future. Resisting arrest was capital, perhaps, but more likely spelled imprisonment. The bleeding statues fraud—he might show that up, if things went hardly with his case—internal troubles might be his salvation. Possibility, however, was death at dawn, blindfolded against a whitewashed wall, or not hooded, but seeing the eyeless circles of the aimed rifles.

His mind was in a muddle, and he could not think straight; as soon as one thing entered his head, another drove it out.

Hard luck, his friends at home had said when plans miscarried, and the plotter was discovered before the bomb exploded; tough to plan, with detail, your retreat and find it blocked, the enemy having known your route, had dug pitfalls and had arranged the land-mines in your path. The mouse the cat did not play with, that had no illusion of having escaped before the velvet claw descended, claws unsheathed.

Now they went down alleys which he had not seen, alleys with walls so high that the sky above seemed a thread. Two guardians went ahead, the rest following. There were doors in the walls, but they seemed to lead to no place; the fat spider made his webs across them and was undisturbed, the wood-worm burrowed knowing that no creosote would kill him, no gas stifle his young in their smaller tunnels. These alleys seemed to be made for secrets; the walls could have no ears, and there were no windows for the peering eyes.

They progressed from alley to alley, crossing wide streets in their course. At last, in the narrowest alley of

88

all, one of the guardians tapped on a web-hung door. Christopher noticed that, although the door was covered with dusty webs, the patch where the guardian knocked was clean and polished, as if by a million knocking hands.

After a minute, not the door, but a section of wall opened sliding apart. They entered a large hall, full, as so many of the halls were, of the antlered heads of giant deer. At the far end, half-hidden in shadow, a man sat in a raised pew.

The guardians marched Christopher down the hall and ushered him into a pew at right angles to that where the man sat. He made himself comfortable on the plush-covered bench.

Suddenly the man on the raised pew spoke: "It is usual to remain on your feet when you are in the presence of a magistrate, Christopher."

Jumping up, Christopher looked at the man, who switched on a floodlight, which showed up his face in detail, as meticulous as a Dutch painting. There sat Omar, still in his leather suit but wearing a mortar-board, as if that added the dignity necessary to a magistrates' bench.

Christopher laughed. "Ha, that was a dirty joke to play on me," he said, "to send out the guradians to arrest me when you only wanted to speak to me. Ha, ha, I suppose you've called me to say you're going to help me get home?"

As he spoke, however, Chris opher saw Omar's face growing more sullen, and felt that there really was trouble ahead. He knew, also, that his laughter sounded forced.

Omar hit the desk in front of him with a small mallet, and shouted, "Silence, Christopher! This, as you will realize, is no laughing matter. You have been caught in the act of plotting to leave the city and, to make matters worse, you committed an assault upon the guardians sent to arrest you. These men were acting under my orders, so, in effect, you are guilty of assaulting me, and, according to the law, that is the same as using violence to *Him*, which is high treason and punishable with death. I would advise you to throw yourself upon the mercy of the court, trusting me to deal leniently with you. If you insist upon your case going up before a judge, you will be dealt with mercilessly and with the full rigour of the law."

Christopher realized that he was in a bad mess, and, then, deciding against throwing himself on Omar's charity, he made up his mind that he would fight the affair out to the very end. It was only by proving his innocence that he would be able to escape. While he was thinking, he sat down again, to the discomfiture of his guards, and anger of Omar; but, before he spoke, he rose to his feet and leaned on the front of the pew.

"Omar," he said, "I demand that, if you insist upon proceeding with this farcical case, I be provided with a lawyer. I do not believe really that you have a case at all. I am a foreigner, and so you have no power over me. I demand that I be deported from your State, with the least possible delay. You have no jurisdiction over my actions, but if you insist upon going on with this stupid game, I claim, as my right, that you arrange for a lawyer for me."

"My dear young man, you may claim what you like as your rights, but I would like to make it clear to you that you have no rights whatsoever. All foreigners must obey our laws while they are here, and, since we are on the subject of foreigners, I would ask you whether you received your card of naturalization before my men arrested you? Ah, ha, you did, I see! Well, then, you are no longer in a position to claim anything *as a foreigner*, having been made a native of this city by special dispensation. You have no rights and no privileges, save those that I, acting as *His* deputy, care to allow you."

90

Christopher took his card from his pocket and held it up. Then, before the guardians could prevent him, he ripped it into pieces and put these fragments into his mouth. They leaped on him, holding him down while they tried to force his mouth open, but when, with the help of a spoon as lever, they finally opened his jaws—not before several fingers had been severely bitten—they removed only an indecipherable mess of papier mâché and gluey pulped buckram.

Rising to his feet again, Christopher shouted at Omar, "That's what I think of your rotten card. Now I haven't got a card I'm all right again, and you have no power over me. I demand that I be set at liberty at once."

Even Omar seemed to be a trifle disconcerted by the foregoing, and was thumbing through a large book which he withdrew from a shelf under his seat. It looked like one of the volumes of *The Proceedings of the Law and Zoological Society*. Having ruffled his way through the pages, he shut the book and tapped again on the wood with his auctioneer's mallet.

"Aukland, known here as Christopher," he said, "I can find no precedent for your outrageous behaviour, and so will need to ask *His* permission to continue your case at a later date, when the legal position has been more clearly defined. I would like you to realize, however, that you have done your case no good by your unconstitutional behaviour. The next time you will be tried in full, and will find that the decision of a judge is not so merciful as that of a magistrate. I, therefore, accede to your wish for a lawyer."

Turning to one of the guardians, he continued, "You will instruct the female official Mali that she is to act as Christopher's custodian during bail, and as his legal representative at his trial."

He rose and removed the mortar-board, as if preparing to leave the room, but Christopher scrambled over the

91

edge of the pew and stood before him, speaking very fast.

"You can't do this, Omar," he gabbled. "You have no evidence to send my case to trial. You must dismiss it now. I plead guilty to having struck a guardian, but also plead extenuating circumstances and provocation. I did not know that it was treason. Apart from that action, I have done nothing wrong—merely tried to sell my own property."

Omar sat down and replaced his mortar-board on his head. "Ah, yes," he said. "The jewels. I'd nearly forgotten them. They will have to be impounded, of course, as essential evidence. Give them to me."

The desert sun for nothing, the mirage gone to waste, jewels brought through time to be taken from me like this. He took a handful of the smaller jewels from one pocket and placed them before Omar.

"These are mine, and I expect you will give them back to me once my innocence has been proved. In the meantime I would like a receipt for them. Where, by the way, can I consult the legal books that will be necessary for the correct conduct of my case?"

"O, my dear Christopher," he was informed affably, "you can't see the legal books, of course. It would not be ethical. No one has ever asked to see them before. Where were you brought up? As for these jewels, they have been impounded as evidence, and anything that is impounded as evidence is no longer your property; automatically it becomes *His* and you have no further claims on it. Are you quite sure you wouldn't like me to have a duplicate card prepared for you, so that you could be content with my verdict on your case? I believe I could, as magistrate, enter the destruction of your card as loss, and you'd only get a short sentence, say six months to a couple of years. Nothing to worry about. Are you sure you wouldn't like me to do that?"

Christopher completely lost his temper, shouting at Omar, and he would have hit the suave smiling face if it had not been out of reach. Omar waited until he paused for breath.

"Well," he said, "I think you'd better be put down for trial. I warn you that all this shouting and abuse will prejudice the judge against you. If you are wise you'll go now. I will give orders to Mali that she is to draw up your plea. Guilty, of course. No one ever pleads not guilty. The case will be fought out just the same on the basis of the length of your sentence. Good-bye for the present. Mind the step."

Looking round, Christopher realized that he was alone with Omar in the court-room. The guardians had gone, and the door into the alley stood open. He gave Omar what he hoped was a scornful glance, and turning round left the room, whistling to himself.

He would show them that they could not get away with this legal travesty. He supposed they thought him an ignorant fellow, knowing nothing, while, in reality, he was the son of a solicitor, and consequently had picked up enough legal gossip to understand the grossly uncon-stitutional nature of their proposals. Of course, the finer points of the law might be different in a strange country, but, on the whole, all laws were the same in that no man could be forced to plead guilty before his trial.

Then he realized that he did not know the nature of the crimes upon which he was to be arraigned, for Omar had spoken of the matter of assault as though it was merely a trivial part of the case. He had not been informed of what it was that he was guilty, and would need to do some research in the matter, for he was damned if he was to be sentenced for an uncommitted offence.

Better, perhaps, to have wandered for ever in the desert, robbed of a future, than to have become the fly in this law's complicated web. It was too much to expect him to prepare a defence without reference to the relevant books, and then there was the trouble about Mali. As she was his counsel, he could not but tell her the truth, without excuse, that he had meant to escape. She might refuse his case, which would add to his difficulties; with no one to guide him in the court procedure, doubtless he would quickly add further offences to his long invisible list.

It was strange to let him out on bail in this way, but he supposed they knew that he could not contrive an escape, and so had no worry for him. Suicide was not yet the way out, for that was possibly a worse captivity than any he had anticipated.

Christopher thought that it looked as though it would take him a long time, indeed, to return to his home, as there seemed to be every likelihood of his receiving a sentence of several years. Had not Omar warned him that, here, a judge was utterly without mercy?

His father, glass in hand, would be at the club at this hour, talking of golf with his cronies; that long shot at the fifth, the neat chip across the remodelled bunker, and the putt that went true from twenty yards against a howling gale. His mother might have friends to tea to discuss the church bazaar, the vicar's weakness for China tea and a trim figure, the vanished husband of a popular neighbour —loss of memory, perhaps, or a younger woman—and the suspected unwarranted birth in the tenements beside the river.

The police would search for him by wireless and small handbills, until his father, weary with much travelling and sick of the sight of bloated corpses, would identify the body washed ashore with the thin wisp of seaweed in the clenched fist, and the hermit-crab ensconced in the withered nostril.

My son would never have done this. Happy at home he would have thought of mother, and remembering her love,

would have returned to us. There has been trickery somewhere, kidnapping, perhaps, or even the sudden call to
adventure. My son, why did you fail me like this? You
were the darling apple of your mother's heart, my prize
pigeon, and my logical successor in the business.

The sentimental and quick kiss, smothering the disgust
rising in the throat, on the cold blue forehead, wrinkled
and eaten by the corrosive waters of the ocean.

Called to the marble-slabbed mortuary, the undertaker
rubs obsequious hands, seeing father, the obviously
prosperous man; measures the coffin with his expert
eye and counts the necessary ornaments, so much a-piece.
Your boy? Mine went out years back. Sheltered beneath
an elm, poor kid, and the forked lightning took him and
left the tree.

Mutual sympathy unties the strings of father's money-
bag, makes him provide a better coffin than his original
intention had ordered. The silver handles will be replaced
by chromium by the undertaker's men, and the plush
lining, while rich within the view of all, is tawdry beneath
the body.

The sad long faces and the slow steps appropriate to
death will go through the cemetery; the black crêpe will
crinkle on the left arm, and the new dark tie, bought for
the occasion, will not lie flat upon the white shirt's bosom.
The few quick words by the graveside, the too-practised
voice of the preacher to whom they have become a
rigmarole, sucked dry by repetition. The sob stopped in
the quavering throat, or else allowed to blossom. Ashes
to ashes.

Then another in his coffin, his grave; his name, Christopher Aukland, carved by the mason, cigarette drooping
from moist lips as the skilled hands fashion each
serif.

I, here, am nothing, and another's body will be mine
for the rest of time. I will not escape now. Forced to stay

here till an old man, with the dribble of senility from my mouth's corner, I will tell the youngsters that I am no native, but one from a far country who became involved in a future not his own. Then, eventually, I suppose, another grave and no mourning. Then two stones with my name, perhaps nearly half a world apart; none will know the solution of my identity and I shall not protest. I can now only go ahead, for there is no retreat.

CHAPTER EIGHT

"CHRISTOPHER, my dear, you are a fool," Mali said. "You must have realized by this time that it's no use trying to escape from this city. You can't get out unless you're sent out, and now you've ruined whatever chance you might have had of leaving. Omar was considering your case carefully, and might have decided to let you go, and have taken me with you. *Might*, I say, because so far as I can remember, no one has ever left the city, save as a prisoner, to work in the clay-pits or the aluminium works. It would only have been a matter of a year or two before Omar had put your case up to *Him*, and *He* had given *His* decision."

"I know I'm a swine, Mali," Christopher replied, "and it's frightfully decent of you not to reproach me for my duplicity, but I hope you'll believe me when I say that it wasn't you I was running away from, but this city with its faceless citizens and unbreakable curfew.

"No one here can see the moon, and they have no knowledge of the stars. The owl can cry as much as it likes and will wake no child, for its long-drawn hoot will not penetrate through concrete walls. The inhabitants know nothing of the appearance of laced branches against a frost-bitten sky, or the sudden scurry of a frightened rabbit from a headlight's glare. Virtually, this is a prison and an actual prison could be no worse. Even in the clay-pits I would be freer than I now am. I would be at liberty to notice the pale lemon spikes of toadflax and the magenta of willowherb, the scarlet of pimpernels, and the blue of butterflies and the many shades of brown of the birds. And, at the least, I would be free of this city."

"That doesn't matter," Mali was saying. "I know that you were not trying to escape from me."

She took Christopher's arm and he sat down beside her and wept, not knowing the reason for his tears, unless it was the wave of futility and exhaustion which beat around him like a tempest.

"My poor sweet," Mali spoke softly and gently, "don't you realize that you have no home now except this city?"

He wept yet more fiercely, angry at the way in which he was being treated by the thing he called fate. It was most unfair that he should have been thrust into this mess, this tangle which he could never hope to unravel.

He had been walking harmlessly down the street. He saw himself, with a throb of self-pity, the polite youth making way for the old women carrying their baskets home from the market. Then there was the explosion, and he wept bitterly for the young man now lying on his back among the shattered stones.

"Come on, Christopher, you really must pull yourself together. This is not the way for us to work out your defence. You know you really do seem to be unlucky, for the judge never gives you less than five years. If you hadn't been so unfortunate and so silly you'd have got off with

97

about six months from the magistrate. Why didn't you plead guilty?"

"Because I'm not guilty of any offence, save the mild one of assault, and I don't even know what other crimes I'm to be accused of. I'm going to prove my innocence."

"You don't realize, my dear, that you are the cause of a great deal of unnecessary trouble. No one here ever pleads not guilty. When you are arrested it's automatically assumed that you are guilty. I'm afraid I won't be able to get you off, for nobody has been discharged within my memory. All I can do is to show your ignorance of our customs, and plead an imperfect acquaintance with the law. Then, perhaps, you will receive the very lightest sentence."

"This is unfair," Christopher shouted, forgetting his self-pity in his indignation. "No civilized country assumes that the prisoner is guilty. The whole business of the law here is a farce, a farce to which I refuse to subscribe. I will appeal."

" Well, of course," Mali replied, thoughtfully chewing a fragment off her thumb-nail, "you *can* appeal, but I would not advise it, as it only means that your sentence will become heavier each time your appeal is dismissed, for, if you're guilty, you've no right to appeal, and you're obviously guilty if you've been brought before the court."

Christopher walked up and down the room, kicking at the fretted chairs. He was caught, as they said, like a rat in a trap. He could not do anything, and was bound to be sentenced under this unjust law. He'd show them, though, that they could not force his acquiescence. He would appeal, and would go on appealing, until he received some satisfaction. There seemed to be no point in making out a case for his innocence, and he told Mali that.

"Ah, my sweet," she said, "I'm glad you're beginning to show some sense at last. That's what I've been trying to make you understand all along. We'll just plead guilty, then they'll give you as light a sentence as the law allows. You know, well-behaved prisoners are allowed to have their wives to visit them, and perhaps even to stay with them. I could come and live with you as soon as things were settled."

"No, Mali, you've got me wrong, I'm afraid. I just meant that it didn't seem to be much use. I did not mean that I'm going to plead guilty. I am not. It's up to them to prove that I'm guilty, and they'll have a job doing it."

"I can't make you out at all, my dear. Just when you seem to be beginning to understand you turn round and get stubborn again. However, it's bed-time now, and I've told you that I'll try and plead ignorance, and we'll just need to hope for the best from that. This time to-morrow we'll know the result."

For a time he forgot his impending trial and was content to realize that Mali was an attractive woman, and that she had her arms around him. After she had fallen asleep, however, he could not rest, and turned uneasily, taking care lest he should disturb her.

He was damned if they were going to drive him to suicide, but that seemed to be the only open road to freedom. He would refuse to work if they sentenced him to the clay-pits, and they could not force him to work with torture. He would resist the sharp agony of the thumb-screw against his nail, and the cracking of his marrowed bones on the rack, rather than submit to an unjust sentence.

When eventually he slept he saw Omar's face smiling at him, growing bigger and then receding just as he was about to hit it. Behind this face he saw the streets of his home town, with the long bright reflections of the arc-lamps on the oily puddles, and the cheerfully-lit tram-cars jolting round corners to the accompaniment of their jangling bells.

He could not return there until, first, he had destroyed the grinning face which blocked his way, dodging his most skilful short-arm jabs and upper-cuts. Now, his wrists were held he could no longer struggle, and Omar was advancing to spit upon him, the venomous expectoration of the toad.

Mali was holding his wrists, and he felt her breath on his face as she spoke, "What is it, darling? It's only me —Mali—it's all right. Don't hit me."

It was daylight and the bulwarks were down. After breakfast he set out with Mali, carrying her brief-case, a bulk composed of few papers but of silk stockings and cosmetics. Their route was the same as his, under escort, the previous day, but they passed the door where the guardian had knocked and turned down a side-alley, the walls of which were covered with crude paintings of an obscene character. Mali paid no attention to these until they came to a particularly obscene group, when she pressed on the nipple of the gross woman who was the central figure.

The wall slid away and they entered a long narrow room, lit by pale blue lamps. They sat down on a couch shaped like a huge swan as the wall closed behind them. Christopher was about to speak when Mali placed a finger before her mouth, pointing to the walls.

Following the direction of her finger, Christopher realized that the knobs which protruded about a foot apart, were not just ornamental bosses, but were microphones, arranged so that the slightest whisper would be conveyed to unseen listeners. He shaped a silent word of thanks to Mali and remained silent, twisting his hands nervously.

Suddenly the couch started moving across the floor and the lights turned to a crimson flame. Christopher would

100

have leaped off the swan, but Mali took his arm to restrain him, remarking, in a normal voice, "It's all right. This is quite usual."

The swan moved quickly, convincing Christopher that they had forgotten to open the doors at the far side. He braced himself to withstand the shock of collision. However, just as the beak of the bird touched the wall, it lifted so quickly that the eye could not follow it, and then, as soon as they were through, dropped behind them with a crash.

The room they entered was decorated in vivid green. At the far end was a bench upon which three figures were seated. As the swan approached Christopher examined them; on the right was a vast effigy of an owl, and on the left, held in place by strings from the roof, a stuffed crocodile, redolent of the alchemist's den.

The central figure was a man, in long scarlet robes trimmed with ermine and wearing a full-bottomed wig. He held a purple ostrich fan so that the feathers covered his face.

At right angles to this bench men were seated, soberly clad in black, with top-hats adorned with crêpe weepers. One or two of these men fidgeted gently with the papers on the desk before them, but the majority were absolutely motionless.

The swan came to a stop, and one of the men barked, "Stand up, prisoner. This, your Lordship, is the prisoner whose case we have been reviewing. He is guilty."

"Who the hell do you think you are to pronounce judgment before I've been tried," Christopher shouted, turning to face the sad-visaged man. "I plead not guilty and demand a proper trial, with a jury of my peers. That is my right."

The judge snorted, and Christopher glanced at him. He moved the plumes which hid his face and disclosed the face of Omar.

"My dear Christopher," he remarked amiably, "how often have I got to remind you that you are no longer in your own country and that, here, you have no rights. You have been tried according to our laws and our legal procedure and have been pronounced guilty. I warned you yesterday that you would be well advised to accept the ruling of the lower courts. I am going to sentence you to eleven years, five months, two weeks and three days' hard labour in the clay-pits. Have you anything to say before I pronounce sentence?"

"Plenty. Why was I not permitted to prepare my defence with the books which you have used for the pro-secution? And why have you arbitrarily arranged that sentence?"

He paused to choke down his anger, and Omar answered him suavely, "We could not let you have the books as they are the property of the courts, and consequently can only be read by those connected with the prosecution, the paid instruments of the court. We used to allow the defence to consult these books, until *He*, in a wise order, forbade it, ruling that it gave the defence an unfair advantage as they were concerned with only one case, while the prosecution always had dozens on hand, and could not therefore devote the same attention to each. As to your sentence—you are fortunate—for I have given you a middle period, that one which coincides with *His* recovery from a serious illness in the year eleven of *His* reign. Have you any further remarks which you wish to make?"

"I wish to appear before the Court of Appeal!"

"My dear boy, there is no Court of Appeal. Of course," slowly and thoughtfully, "you can, if you wish, appeal to the Chancellor, but that is a course I really cannot advise you to take. It is a course that is almost bound to lead to disaster, for, as is fitting, he has a sense of humour and might set you to do the most impossible things. You

102

should accept my lenient sentence, and I will give orders to the effect that, instead of the one day per year that is customary, you be given two days remission in respect of good conduct. Naturally, however, if you are a troublesome prisoner, you will find your sentence increased, at the rate of one month per misdemeanour. Do you now wish to accept my very generous offer?"

"No. I appeal to the Chancellor!"

Immediately the whole court was in an uproar. A little man, tripping over the weepers from his top-hat, ran up to Christopher and exclaimed, "You're very foolish, you know. It is almost unprecedented." Christopher swept him aside and turned towards Mali, to see why she had not supported him.

She was lying stretched on the swan in a passionate embrace with one of the black-clad men. The man's top-hat was tilted back on his head. Christopher walked over to him and, deliberately, smashed it down over his face. Mali did not slacken her embrace, and the man lifted a hand and removed the shattered hat. As he was doing this, Mali's eyes met those of Christopher, but she showed no recognition of him. He might have been one of the obscene paintings on the wall outside for all the interest she showed in him.

Christopher stood looking down at her for a moment, and then, slowly and heavily, walked across to the officials' desk. He swept the papers from it into a bundle. It was like a slow-motion film. A man lifted his hand to stop him, ever so slowly, as Christopher's hand slid, crabwise, along the desk, just a fraction before it, closing like a claw round the neat bundles of stiff paper. He stepped back, his foot moving through the air like a giant crane, as the man's hand came gradually towards him.

Out of reach of the man, Christopher began tearing the papers up. As he did so he saw the black-clothed men advancing slowly, oh so slowly! from every corner

103

of the court. A large bundle of scraps lay at his feet. Christopher stooped and scooped up the pile and, like a dancer, lifted his arms above his head and the bits of paper fell slowly past him, as snowflakes past a tree.

As the last scrap flickered to the ground things resumed their normal speed. Christopher found his elbows grabbed by two of the black-clad men, while a third, and Christopher recognized him as the little man who had spoken to him earlier, danced in front of him, crying, "Most unconstitutional, my man, most unconstitutional. You'll pay for this, my man, just see if you don't! Disgraceful scene —never seen the like in all my life. What do you mean by your behaviour, my man?"

Gathering a great gob of spittle in front of his teeth, Christopher expectorated violently into the face of the little man, who ran away, exclaiming, "You've blinded me, my man, you'll pay for this, just see if you don't!"

The two who held Christopher's arms laughed heartily at their colleague's discomfort, and Christopher, thinking it might be well to keep on their good side, started to laugh with them, hoarsely and without humour. Immediately he started to laugh, however, they stopped, looking at one another. Then they twisted his arms up behind his back, until the pain was so severe that he nearly cried out.

Once he was silent they loosened his arms and held them stiffly down by his sides. He looked round the hall to see that Omar had gone, but that his companions of the bench, astonished owl and supercilious crocodile, remained in their places. Most of the black-clad men were down on their knees trying to piece together the torn fragments of paper, an impossible jigsaw puzzle, shaking their heads gravely and hopelessly as they bent to their task. Mali still lay clutched in the embrace of the man whose shattered hat lay on the floor beside them.

104

The men who held Christopher led him down the hall, and as he reached the swan couch he stopped, and they, too, stopped as if wondering what he thought he could do. They kept a firm grip on his elbows, but seemed to have forgotten that he still had control of his legs, and so permitted him to manœuvre himself into a favourable position, from which he lashed out at the tightly stretched seat of the recumbent man's trousers.

The man released his hold on Mali, who fell back on to the swan, bumping her head on the wooden moulding. Christopher looked down at her, ignoring the curses of her discomfited lover, to see that she had genuinely forgotten all about him. He stared into her blank eyes, failing to gather even the faintest glimmer of recollection there, and he doubted whether the finest actress would have been able to glean the last straw of memory from eyes that covered a mind with sheaves of reminiscence. After all, they said, it was not in his behaviour that one traced the yellow streak in a man's heart, but in his eyes, eyes which wishes could not shutter.

They went on down the hall, slowly yet smartly, like a squad at a funeral. Would the Last Post suddenly sound as they walked, to be followed by the dull echo of the shots, the final salute? It would seem unlikely, for Christopher lacked companions to perform these good offices for him, and was alone, forgotten even by the woman whose embraces he had returned so fervently the previous night, a night as far behind him as the dawn of history.

At the far end of the hall they halted for a moment, and Christopher felt his two guards stiffen as if in readiness to receive an expected blow. Then the wall before him opened and he was thrust through the gap. The two black lawyers drew back while the wall closed and once again he was alone in a tiny room. His compartment started to sway, and he realized that he was in a lift, and that he was travelling swiftly upwards; his stomach felt as if it had been cleared by a strong and violent purge, and the pressure of the air made his head sing. It was quite three minutes before the lift stopped its upward surge.

Christopher looked at the wall through which he had entered, waiting for it to open for his exit. Suddenly he heard a voice behind him, an affable wheedling, oily voice. He wheeled round. "Ah, ha, my dear Christopher! Surely you've learned to distrust the obvious by this time?"

Behind him, the wall of the lift had opened, and Omar stood in the doorway, not the lean suave Omar of the judges' bench, but an Omar whose face was crackled with his smiles, and who seemed to have been stuffed with cushions to give him a Falstaffian corpulence, on the principle that fat men are good-humoured men.

" You're not the Chancellor, are you?" Christopher gasped. "I wanted to appeal to the Chancellor—not to you! I wanted to escape from your legal sophistries and prejudice. I asked only for a stated case and a fair trial."

Omar wheezed, "Yes, my dear boy, I'm the Chancellor. I'm the big boss himself. How are you, my dear fellow? Feeling quite well after a journey in my private lift? Now, now, don't be bad tempered—let us retain our equanimity and discuss this affair of yours in as amicable a fashion as is possible. Won't you have a glass of wine, or perhaps a drop of whisky and soda? What! No? Well, well, if that's how you feel I suppose there's nothing I can do to add to your comfort. But perhaps you are a convert to teetotalism, a rechabite—a refuser of hairs of the dog—a wretched fellow? No? Then it's very strange that you should refuse a drink, for, without any boasting, I can claim that this is the best wine in the city. You're being foolish in refusing my offer of even a small glass. Most people would be glad of the chance of sampling my

106

cellar. Ah, that's better. Say when. I rather thought you'd be reasonable after a little wheedling talk from your old Uncle Omar."

Christopher had jerked his head in irritation, and before he had had time to protest again Omar had produced glasses, and a long slender bottle, and was deep in the ritual of dealing out wine, a religious ceremony needing a white cloth slung over the left forearm. The neat twist of the hand as he drew out the cork and the ease with which he held the bottle to fill the two glasses showed the priest of the performance to be no neophyte.

Omar sat down on a large cushion and beckoned Christopher to another. As there did not seem to be anything else to do, Christopher sat down and lifted his glass to his lips. It might have been water for all the taste he savoured as he sipped.

He started to speak, but Omar held up a hand to indicate that they should remain silent as they drank their wine. During this lull Christopher looked around him. The room was arched by a dome of pale blue glass with a large electric violet-ray lamp in the centre, in a setting made of gilded wood carved in the form of the points of a star, but obviously representing the sun. The walls and woodwork were of a pale yellow, but were hidden for the most part by the pictures which covered every flat surface; all these pictures were obscene, running from huge, unwieldy giants in gilt frames to pretty miniature water-colours in frames of filagree silver and cloacial coarse drawings, exhibiting neither dexterity of hand nor anatomical knowledge, held in place with drawing-pins.

When they had drunk their wine, Omar leaned back and placed the tips of his fingers together, examining the thick nails with the intensity of a connoisseur. Then he yawned once or twice and smiled gently as if at some private joke, a cat's smile without apparent feeling or meaning for the spectator.

"Ah, Christopher!" he said, "you know you really have been a nuisance. It is just as well for you that, in my sentimental way, I have taken a liking to you. For, as you realize by this time, nothing could be easier than for me to order your immediate execution." He sighed heavily. "Many's the time I have upraided myself for my foibles, my emotional quirks. But, ah, my boy! you will understand that sometimes I have to steel my unwilling, you don't know how unwilling, heart and order the extermination of a favourite—for the good of the State. If I had to order your execution, my dear Christopher, I would feel it as bitterly as a man feels the death of his favourite spaniel, condemned perhaps for sheep killing or some other crime of a like nature. I don't like to think of the words 'execution' or 'extermination' in connexion with you. Rather I'd say you were being 'put down' or 'sent to sleep.' "

"What for?" enquired Christopher. "I haven't done anything against your State, have I? I merely wanted to leave this city and go home. That's no crime in any decent country."

Omar paid no attention to this protest and went on: "Now you know it really was very naughty of you to tear up all the lawyers' papers. I could make things very *awk*ward for you, Christopher *Auk*land, ha, ha! say by putting you up to *auc*tion as a slave, ha, ha! but I have my reputation to think of here. The Chancellor is a humourist, ha, ha! and makes the punishment fit the crime and the criminal."

He leaned back and started to roar with laughter, an empty laughter as meaningless as the noise produced by hitting a hollow brass statue of Buddha with a broomstick. At length, with a vast show of difficulty, he took a huge lemon-yellow silk handkerchief and wiped his dry eyes with a corner of it.

"As I say, I've a reputation to foster, and so I've done

108

a lot of thinking about your case. Naturally, your punishment will be pretty arduous as a consequence of the amount of work I've put into it. So you like snowstorms, do you? What do I mean? Why, you played snowstorms with the lawyers' papers, so I'll play snowstorms with you. Ha, ha, ha, ha!"

Christopher did not like the sound of this laughter at all, and waited with a dull heavy feeling in the pit of his stomach for Omar to continue. "So your name is *Auk*land, eh? Well, you can go and hunt a Great *Auk* for me. You'll get plenty snowstorms by the way, I'll wager."

"This is ridiculous. You can't do it. It isn't legal and it isn't even common justice!" Christopher burst out. He felt that he had got into the hand of a madman, and cast hurried glances around him, trying to find some way of escape.

"It's no use looking round you like that, you can't get out," Omar remarked, his voice as level as a Flemish landscape. "And, by the way, I'd like you to realize that I'll do as I damned well like with you. You might as well be grateful for the lenience I've shown and shut your mouth."

He started to laugh again, more heartily than ever, and Christopher had to shout at the top of his voice to penetrate the hard brittle waves of empty sound, "I call your bluff, Omar. I appeal to *Him!*"

At this Omar became almost hysterical, rocking backwards and forwards with his hands clutching his hollow façade of belly. It almost looked as though he might fall over.

Suddenly he was silent. He leaned forward and touched Christopher on the knee.

"You can't," his voice was hushed and confidential, the great surgeon announcing the existence of an incurable cancer to the patient's nearest relations, "and I wonder

109

if you'd like to know why? My question, as you will gather, is rhetorical—I mean to tell you! It is a very closely guarded secret, but you won't be able to make use of it. I'm *Him*. There you are, my boy, you're beaten and you might as well admit it. There's nothing you can do about the matter. You'll just have to go off and take a look around for the Great Auk. I'm afraid you'll find it a bit of a job, as the last one was killed a hundred years ago. However, you may have luck, and, as I'm a decent sporting sort of fellow, I'll see to it that you are given the necessary equipment to give you a fair chance.

"Fancy you thinking that you could get above me. I've never heard of anything so funny in all my life. Who did you think *He* was? Couldn't you guess that *He* had no existence beyond and within me, that I'm the king-pin, the big shot, the boss, the chief, the master, the director, or what you will, here? Since you will not be able to do any harm now, I don't mind telling you that I have found *Him* an extremely useful figurehead, my private whipping boy. You know, *He* is the source of all the unpopular laws, and when a popular reform is announced, it is yours truly that takes the credit—always thinking of the good of the people. However, what I say in this country goes, and you can't alter that!"

"I'll be judge, I'll be jury, said cunning old Fury," Christopher muttered. Omar took it as a compliment and insisted on pouring out another glass of wine, saying, "Here's to the success of your venture. If you find the Great Auk, I don't know what'll happen to you. You may be allowed to go home—or you may receive a position as an Official here. However, there's no need for me to worry about that at the moment. Good-bye, my dear boy."

He rose to his feet, ringing a bell as he spoke, and held out his hand, an explorer greeting a friend about to explore the upper reaches of a Nile or Amazon.

Christopher made as though he was going to seize the outstretched hand of comradeship, his face benign with lack of malice, and then, as guards poured into the room on all sides, he smashed his balled fist up at Omar's nose. He had the satisfaction of hearing and feeling the little bones crunch beneath the impact, before the guards rushed forward to seize his arms.

Crimson blood trickled from the already bulbous tip of Omar's nose, but his equanimity did not desert him. He drew towards him the pad on which he had been jotting, scratched out one word with a steady stroke of the pen and substituted another above it. "That," he remarked without bitterness, "was merely a display of foolishness. I cannot disregard it, with the best will in the world. I have changed your sentence from one Great Auk to a brace. I fear that you will not fulfil the conditions, and I am sorry for you. Take him away."

As they climbed down a spiral staircase Christopher felt that his interview with Omar had not been real, the whole affair had the terrifying unlogical logic of a dream. Perhaps, in a few minutes, he would wake to find himself back at home, and to hear the pettish voice of his mother calling that she was about to clear away the breakfast, and he would get none if he did not hurry up.

But the men who held his arms seemed to be very real, and the pain from the half-Nelson one of them had put on his right arm was not the sort of pain suffered in dreams, even when sleeping in the most unnatural position.

There was no doubt about it, the things that were happening to him were real, improbable though they might appear, and he could do nothing to slow down the tempo of his actual nightmare.

Omar had said that he would be supplied with the equipment he needed for his search, and that equipment might include the things he would find necessary for

111

travel homeward, rather than to the fringes of polar ice in search of an extinct bird.

However, he would be free during his search for the bird, free of this unreal city with its too well defined laws and its dictator. He could try and escape once out in the country more easily than he could in the town.

At the foot of the spiral staircase a door opened in the wall and Christopher was thrown on his face into a room exactly the same as that he had occupied on the night he had entered the city.

He lay on the spongy rubber floor, cursing himself for the direction he had taken to lead him out of the desert. If only he had gone across the flat sands he would probably have arrived safely at his home. He had taken the wrong turning, and there was no side-road for him to try. He could only go on now, on to some end that he did not know and did not dare to imagine.

CHAPTER NINE

RAIN fell continually from the unburnished sky, and underfoot the ground was wet and boggy. If you slipped in the least your boots became full of peaty water, and the fibres from the roots twined themselves round your toes, and were as cutting as the finest silken threads. No one spoke and it was hard on the nerves.

Often, walking through thin swirls of mist, it was all that Christopher could do to see his escort, five paces behind and five in front, but he knew that they were watching him, and if he had tried to make a bolt for it would have brought him headlong. The lame hare shot as it dodged among the snarls of heather, its smoking fur rotting under the perpetual dampness. The solitary sheep, seen one dawn upon a little hill, as large in the deceptive mist as a cathedral, its horns twin Gothic spires. The sad cry of a curlew magnified by the bowl-reflectors of the hills until it sounded like the crying of all the damned souls in human history.

It was just a matter of keeping one's eyes fixed on one's boots and the little patch of ground just ahead. Sometimes a blind-worm slithered quickly out of reach of the aimed boot or ready stick, sometimes a stoat slipped rapidly across the path. Sometimes a corncrake grated in the distance, or a trapped animal shrieked in agony. A skua a little distance from the roadside lapped at the entrails of a still living lamb.

All these did not count; they were as far removed from life as an ammonite in a museum. Christopher felt he had the dead for company, the slow breathing of the guards as they slogged along was as mechanical as the puffing of a steam engine.

Once or twice he tried to break through the curtains around him by singing, a defiant shout in the immense vacuum, but they paid no attention to this, and he soon stopped as his voice came back to him, echoed from the wall of dampness, a distorted caricature of the words flung out so bravely. Another time he stumbled and fell, crying out in pain as his knee struck a snag of bog-oak, but a guard pulled him to his feet and they went on again, in silence.

Christopher started counting his footsteps out loud, but the sound of his voice and the monotony of the action made him feel as though he was going mad. He turned to the captain in charge of his escort, his voice breaking as he spoke, "Look here, do we need to be as silent as this? I don't know how much longer I can stand it. Say something, damn you! Speak!"

The captain shook his head, and as they went on the silence seemed the more intense because of his outbreak, emphasized by the sounds common to the moors. A hare the size of a cow loomed through the mist, and a grouse started up like a bomber diving.

He knew that his companions were not dumb, for occasionally he heard a word pass between two of them, but, when he turned to see who had spoken, all the faces were as blank as the shells of eggs, and none of them responded to his entreaties.

They went on, and on, and on, and it seemed to Christopher that the very sky wept for him, little moist tears of misery for him in his unfortunate situation.

Perhaps Omar had decided that he would keep him walking till he dropped from exhaustion into one of the bogs, where he would sink slowly, his mouth filling with the brackish water, making vain efforts to spit out the tangled bitter roots of the marsh-marigolds and bog-beans. He would lie there, deep in the black peat till his bones became like the roots of the bog-oak which shone like ebony, and all his flesh had become one fatty rancid mass.

Sometimes the flush of self-pity became so uncontrollable that he felt he could cry, and then he saw himself, the badly treated little man, always thinking of himself as little, marching for ever under a damp sky with a silent escort. The little man who had been caught in the driving belt of the law through no fault of his own, and who was now, as they said, damned to a fate worse than death. When he saw himself like that Christopher felt two heavy tears rolling down the creases on either side of his nose, and he put out his tongue to catch them, salty and sour on the tip, pleased with himself for this little private display of his dexterity.

He felt slightly more cheerful, and started looking round him with greater interest. Despite the mist and drizzle, the moor was better than that town with its false concrete walls hiding the Gothic houses. It was rather pleasant, when the haze lifted, to see for miles across the heather, knowing that he was at least free of the immediate jurisdiction of Omar.

It was a pity that his escort would not talk, but if they were determined to remain silent, well, he would not interfere with them. He wondered how much further they would go before they rested, and before they gave him something to eat, for he had not touched food since early morning and felt hungry. It was all very well for his guards to keep on going, for he noticed that they refreshed themselves as they went, extracting blocks of chocolate and ham-sandwiches from their leather pouches, but no one offered him so much as a bite.

The captain was occupied in peeling a banana with maddening slowness and precision. Christopher let his paces drag slightly, so that although he did not appear to slow down he was soon only a pace or two in front of the captain. Looking out of the corner of his eye, he could see the skin of the banana being turned down neatly by accurate fingers, and felt that it was very unfair of the captain to parade his food in that manner.

Suddenly Christopher leaned back, just as the hand raised the phallic fruit towards the lips, and snatched it away to shovel it into his own mouth. He waited for the burst of imprecation he expected from the captain, but all he said was, "Hungry, eh? Why didn't you say so before?"

"You didn't give me much of a chance to say I was hungry, did you?" Christopher replied. "Of course I'm hungry. Wouldn't you be famished if you'd been going all day and hadn't had a bite? What can you expect?"

115

The captain did not answer but beckoned to his men. They halted and started to erect a large collapsible tent which four of them carried, setting up a canvas table inside it. Several of them unslung large boxes from which they produced roast beef, potatoes and brussels sprouts, kept hot in glass containers. The food was ladled out on to two plates and the men withdrew, leaving Christopher and the captain to sit down on three-legged stools and start eating.

Christopher did not say anything, but concentrated on eating with the utmost ferocity, as if half afraid that they would suddenly whip the food away from him if he hesitated. After the meal the men produced mugs full of hot coffee, and the captain held out a cigarette case.

"How do you feel now?" he enquired. "Better for that? I hope you didn't think it rude of me not replying to your questions all day, but I was ordered to hold no conversation with you until you asked for food. I think it was a bit hard on you, but I couldn't help it. *His* orders, you know, and *He* must be obeyed."

"Oh, that's all right," Christopher answered. "But of course you don't know who *He* is, do you? *He's* nobody else than Omar. I got that straight from the horse's mouth, from the jaws of Omar himself."

The captain looked half-interested for a moment, and Christopher thought he was about to enter into conversation on the subject, but when he spoke his voice was that of the reasoned reply to the querulous child: "Nonsense. That kind of remark is treasonable. I expect you'll want to go to bed now?"

In the morning, after breakfast, they went on again. Before the start the captain turned to Christopher, saying, "Awfully sorry, old chap, but I've got to obey orders, and so we can't speak again till you're hungry. Red tape and all that, of course, but I'm an officer, and so I must obey orders or get into the most frightful trouble. I hope

116

you won't make it too hard for me, and that you'll understand my position. I know it must be pretty filthy for you to have to travel all day without saying a word, but I can't help it."

The guards fell in again, and now the mist had lifted a little, Christopher could see that he really would have no chance whatsoever if he tried to make a break for freedom. The guards were deployed a few feet apart, about thirty yards away on each side of him, so that his wings were effectively blocked and both before and behind him there marched a compact body of men, sub-machine guns under their arms, who looked as though they would bring him down without any hesitation if he looked like escaping.

A watery sun shone through the white mist overhead, and the drops of dew on the olive green of the bog-myrtle shone and glittered, and the spiders' webs sparkled as if they had been wrought of platinum and set with brilliants. When he thought of jewels, Christopher remembered that, for all their efficiency, none of the guards he had encountered had bothered to search him, and running his hands over his pockets furtively he assured himself that he still had his handfuls of uncut stones.

He wondered what the captain of the guard got in the way of wages, and whether it would be worth while trying to bribe him in an effort to discover the best way to his home. It would certainly be easier to get home by tramping across moorland than by sea, as he would be certain to find food on the moors while on the sea he would be dependent on the fish he caught, and though Omar had promised him the equipment needed to see the Great Auk, he had said nothing about fishing tackle.

He tried to remember all that he could about the Great Auk, but the total of his knowledge was not great. The last of the Gair Fowl (for that was the Great Auk's other name, its mirror self) had, as Omar said, been killed above

117

a hundred years ago, and somewhere in the story of its death there was a reminiscence of witchcraft, a reminiscence on which he could not put his finger. It was an ungainly creature out of the water, for its short stumps of wings would not permit it to fly, but in the water it travelled with the speed of an ocean liner and as sleekly as a seal. Its eggs and stuffed skin were the prizes of the zoologist and ornithologist, their value being dependent upon the fact that it was extinct. That word, the word "extinct," showed that he had been sent upon as hopeless a venture as he could well imagine. He might as well have been set to report upon the other side of the moon, or to enumerate the multitudinous stars.

He counted the jewels in his pockets, pretending to feel for a handkerchief, and found that he still had somewhere about thirty of different sizes. In his breast pocket he could feel the shiny backs of the bronze ladybirds from the last cactus of the timeless desert. He managed to slip one into the palm of his hand, and looked at it as it lay cupped there, admiring the sheen of the red wing-cases with their minute black spots, half expecting them to open and the little beetle to vanish on its celophane wings. "Ladybird, ladybird," he murmured, "fly away home, your house is on fire and your children all gone. Come on, hurry up before I regret my impulse to let you go. Oh, so you want to stay, do you? Very well, back you can go into my pocket, and I hope you will not regret your captivity."

He had, apparently been speaking louder than he had realized, for as he slid the bronze beetle back into his breast pocket, to join the others, the captain of the guard drew level with him. He said nothing, but looked at Christopher in the doubtful manner of one who has approached a bull without first ascertaining its mental condition.

The captain took a block of chocolate from his pocket,

and breaking off a fragment handed it to Christopher, who said, "As we're eating, I don't see any reason why we should continue in silence, do you? Is there anything about that in the rules?"

"Well, now you mention it," the captain replied, "I don't think there is, and so I don't see any reason against our talking. How are you feeling?"

Christopher felt in his side-pocket and closed his fingers round the largest jewel he could find. Then he spoke, "Oh, I'm all right, though I do think this march is a bit of an unnecessary farce. I say, I was just wondering when you came up whether they pay you officers at all well?"

"That, as a matter of fact, is one of our grievances. We get very little more than an ordinary guardian, and yet, if things go wrong, we are held to be responsible. It's a jolly bad show, in fact, and something will have to be done about it soon if they think they're going to get any more officers. I know of several youngsters who were put down for the guardians, but who've recently changed their minds and gone in for ordinary official posts. There's some chance of a promotion for them there, and they start at the wage a captain reaches after twenty years' service. I can tell you there's a good many people taking a pretty poor view of the whole business."

Christopher thought this was just the sort of grumble he wanted, and slipped the jewel into the captain's hand, saying, "Look here, get what you can for this. It'll be more use to you than to me. If you'd care to do it, I suppose you could go home and say you'd put me out to sea, when all the time you'd let me get away across the moors? No one would be any the wiser. If you could do this, I might be able to tell you where you'd get a lot more of these jewels, so that you'd be able to get quite rich."

The captain pocketed the jewel with an adroit move-

119

ment designed to hide his acquisition from the too sharp eyes of his men.

"I'm awfully sorry, old chap," he replied, "I can't possibly do what you want. You see, I've got to deliver you safe and sound at the Penal Settlement at North Point, and they do all the arranging for your expedition there. They'll have received full particulars of your case by this time, and so, if you're not in their hands by midday to-morrow they'll send out search parties to look for you. Even if I let you go you wouldn't have the slightest chance of getting away, for they've got aeroplanes there and would spray every inch of the countryside with poison gas, and the mustard would soon percolate through your boots to make walking a physical impossibility.

"All the same, it's frightfully decent of you to give me this jewel. Do you know what I'll do with the proceeds? I'll tell you. I'll change my girl. Up to now I've never been able to afford a proper first-grade woman, and sometimes I've even been forced to make do with an ordinary citizeness. You know, they do say that all cats are grey after dark, but still it's a bit disturbing to wake up in the night and think that the head on the pillow beside you hasn't got a face. If there should be anything else that I could do for you, please let me know what it is. I'm really frightfully upset about you, for you seem to be the right sort of chap—not at all the usual bounder that we have to escort to the Penal Settlement. That was a bright idea of yours about the chocolate. If we eat it slowly, we can walk along talking till it's time to pitch camp for the night."

Christopher felt annoyed with himself for giving up his biggest stone with no return. It suddenly occurred to him that he might as well have the satisfaction of revenging himself on Mali for her forgetfulness of him. He said, "You know, they gave me a first-grade woman. Her name is Mali. You should try and get hold of her. She lives with citizens W and Y, and, believe me, she's a hot bit of stuff."

He pitched his voice in the correctly hearty and confidential tone of one regular fellow to another.

"Thanks awfully. I must remember her name," said the captain, jotting a memorandum on the flap of his revolver-holster. Christopher thought, it serves her right if she is bored to death by this chap, and he felt so pleased with himself that he gave the captain two of the smaller stones to make certain that he would have enough money to buy himself a place in Mali's favours. The captain showed no curiosity about the source of the jewels, but tucked them away in his pockets. They walked on in silence, the captain presumably tasting the pleasures that were to be his when he had sold the jewels.

Christopher felt that he had never had such perfect eyesight in all his life; he had X-ray eyes that could penetrate the thickest mist and could almost see the worms underground. He could concentrate on the gummy hairs on the little round red leaves of the sundew, and the almost microscopic insects that were caught there. A curlew passed ahead of them as fast as its driving wings would take it, and Christopher was convinced that he saw the thin line that marked the division in the slender beak and the slight disarray of certain feathers was as obvious as if he had held the bird in his hand.

He felt that in a few minutes more he would be able to see the future as clearly and as sharply. He would see what it was that he was travelling towards. He would see his end, whether it lay at home, the traveller returned after his hardships and his hairbreadth escapes to die quietly in a comfortable bed with the pillow smooth and none of the clothes disarranged, or whether it would happen in the north, the small boat crushed by the affectionate ice and the traveller starving on the blue berg, or, perhaps, the sudden swell that would overthrow him, to swim for hours until at last he forgot to swim and felt the water flow through his lungs as easily as the air to which they were accustomed.

He did not want to see the future. It might be too painful and it would not be so easy to believe and accept an end which one saw mapped out before one. He stumbled on a tuft of heather and the thud of his head against a knob of springy turf woke him from his vision, and once more things were blurred as normal.

The captain was talking: "So you see, I'm afraid I can't help you. Your only chance is to try and find your way home by sea. I don't think you've much chance like that, but still, you'll be on your own, and you'll know that there is no one looking at you the whole time."

It really would be rather a sell for Omar if Christopher turned up carrying a brace, or whatever a pair was called, of Great Auks, and solemnly presented them to him. Omar would not know what to say, and would perhaps give him his freedom from sheer surprise. For the present, however, the sea lay ahead of him, and the future was crusted with its barnacles of danger.

The mist was thickening, and it had started to rain again, but still they showed no signs of halting. Christopher was glad that his leather coat was waterproof, as otherwise he would have been wet through, but he wished that the pathway had not become so slippery. Several times he just saved himself from falling by clutching at the captain's arm, and he wondered how it was that the guardians did not seem to slide until he noticed that the soles of their boots were barred like those of footballers, and that the butts of their rifles were fitted with short spikes, like miniature bayonets at the wrong end.

In the evening they pitched camp beneath a tall rock. Christopher and the captain ate without talking, and retired to bed almost immediately after. Christopher lay awake for a long time, listening to the regular breathing of the captain who, he thought, was probably occupied by voluptuous dreams with himself as hero of the harem.

Christopher himself woke again before dawn and lay on his side looking at the wall of the tent growing lighter as the sky outside lightened with the rising sun. He tried not to think of anything that was not enclosed in the present moment and visible to his eyes. He was in a tent set nowhere in particular with nothing outside it. He looked at the tent poles until he felt that he could have drawn every splinter accurately.

The captain lay on his back. His mouth was open and the edge of the sheet lay across it, rising and falling as he sucked and blew. His yellow hair was towsled, and locks of it dangled over his brow. He did not seem to have anything to worry over, and his open mouth seemed to be laughing.

However, Christopher noticed, he had flung his right hand above the blankets, and round his wrist was bound a slender lanyard, the other end of which had pulled the black squat butt of a revolver into sight.

They ate, chatting about trivialities such as the weather and the common animals of the countryside, and then started off again, the captain assuring Christopher that they were less than a half-day's march from the Penal Settlement. They seemed to be climbing up the side of a mountain, for the track became more clearly defined, and wound upward in a spiral.

The gradient was never very steep, and Christopher felt that he would not have noticed it at all except for the increased rarity of the air. The guardians were puffing and he realized the coldness, seeing the gusts of breath as clouds of steam against the red faces and frosty blue noses.

The mist cleared into swirls, the blown hair of a ghost,

and soon, several miles ahead of them, they saw a gathering of buildings, the glaring white of an Arab city across the desert.

The captain offered Christopher a segment of milk chocolate, saying, "There's the Penal Settlement. The sea is down a cliff on the far side, and the prisoners make salt from the water or hew blocks of granite from the cliffs. Don't be surprised if the man that meets you seems to be familiar. It's Omar's son, and he got this job as it's one of the best in the country—when you've had it five years you've made enough to retire on—and he looks just like his father. He's not a bad chap once you get to know him. We were at school together, and I will say that he never gave himself airs. Naturally, he took this job when his father offered it—he's as keen as the rest of us on the flesh-pots—and, as a matter of fact, when he retires, which will be in rather less than a year, he's promised to recommend me as his successor."

"It must be pretty dull to be stuck up here," Christopher remarked, "so far from the town and everything to do with it. Though I can't say that *I* found your town very invigorating myself."

"Dull!" exclaimed the captain. "Not on your life! They give you a woman and a wonderful house, and you choose the best prisoners as your servants. I'm not surprised you found the town dull. You need to have some influence to get into the night clubs. I've been there once or twice, and the things I saw—why, you'd never believe them! Young Omar took me one time, and as he'd just had a bit of a to-do with the governor he showed me what the old man did in his spare time. The room was just a tangled mass of nudity!"

Looking as if he had said too much, the captain shut up suddenly like a mussel approached by a questing stick. Christopher tried to encourage him to continue, promising that anything he heard would go no further.

124

The captain went on, "Of course, if Omar knew that I'd seen through the peep-hole, he'd have had me reduced to the ranks at once. He would have been livid, as no one, not even young Omar, is supposed to know that he frequents those places. The funny thing is that nearly all the official class have a pretty fair idea of what he does when he's out of sight, but they daren't say anything or there might be a complete reversal. The citizens might be made into officials, and then the officials would have to work. And I know that Omar'd do that if he felt like it. Of course, it would be an awfully foolish move, as it would be sure to lead to a revolution, and there's no telling where a revolution will end. They might even try to overthrow Omar, and then there'd be a fine kick-up. I may be a guardian officer and all that, but no wars for yours truly is my motto. Too much blood and no security."

While they had been talking they had been drawing nearer to the white cluster of buildings. Now Christopher could make out some small figures working at one of the walls. He kept his eyes on them, and soon he could make out that one of them was writing letters in black paint on the wall. The letters were so tired and straggling that at first he could not make them out, but gradually they formed words, and he read, "I am a traitor."

The man who was writing these words was followed by two others, who were making every effort, with scrubbing brushes and water, to remove the paint. The men were all, in spite of the bite in the air, dressed only in shorts, and as the escort drew level, one of the watching warders slashed one of the men across the bare shoulders with a vicious thin-lashed whip, leaving a streak of blood oozing from the welt he raised. He then took the man and, smashing his head brutally against the white concrete wall, roared, "Do you call that clean? Hurry up and do your work properly, if you don't want a flogging."

The man turned a thin, white, tightly-drawn face up. Christopher could not restrain the step he took towards the warder, but before he had time to say or do anything, two of the guardians seized his arms and the captain hissed, "Shut up, you fool. You're my prisoner and you'll get the same if you interfere. What did these men do? They took part in a rising to find out the proper name of *Him*, and this is their punishment. Come on now, be a good chap and pull yourself together. I've taken quite a liking to you, and I wouldn't like anything bad to overtake you. Young Omar is watching us through his telescope, and if I give a good report of you, and he doesn't see anything to contradict my opinion, he'll treat you quite decently. After all, your punishment is not the sort they give to a serious offender. You've got off pretty lightly."

Christopher began, "Lightly, eh? That's a funny word to use when I've been set to do the impossible." Before he had time to embroider this theme, however, the party was challenged by a man in a pale blue silk uniform, riding a tractor, who had a machine-gun mounted on a swivel before him.

The captain advanced, presenting his credentials, and spoke a few words of explanation to the man who hesitated briefly, until a voice behind him bawled, "Don't dawdle, you bloody fool, I'm expecting them." The man in uniform muttered under his breath, and then said quietly, "Go ahead, you bastards, his royal chamber-pot awaits your bloody arrival."

Christopher waited for someone to rebuke the man, but no one did, and they went forward towards the voice, which had seemed to come from a grating in a large steel door which shone like a mirror, reflecting their approach, so that they seemed to be advancing to meet another party.

This door was drawn upward, and they entered a large hall. On a flight of marble steps at the far end, a woman hanging on his arm, Omar Junior awaited their arrival, the host expectant for the honoured guests.

The captain walked up the hall with the definite steps of one who had done the same thing often before. "Hello, Juney," he said, "how's yourself? Here's my prisoner, Christopher Aukland. A decent chap, you know, but he seems to have got across your old man, even to the extent of dotting him one on the beak, so he's in the soup. Have you got orders about him?"

"Ah, yes, Rolfe, my dear fellow, I got word yesterday. If you say he's a decent fellow there's no reason why he shouldn't eat with us. Probably be the last decent meal the poor chap'll see for a good long time. Pleased to meet you. Sorry about all this trouble. The old man's got an odd sense of what's funny, and it's not wise to cross him, as you'll know by this time. I suppose that you'd like a good clean up before anything?"

He clapped his hands and a man came forward from the side of the hall. He, like the rest of the prisoners, was naked except for a pair of shorts, but, unlike those Christopher had previously seen, he had the letter T branded on his chest, a horrible purple plummy wound.

This prisoner led Christopher down a corridor and entered a room fitted up as a barber's shop. Another prisoner was already there who beckoned to Christopher to strip. He started to do so, and the two men lifted a section of flooring to reveal a large square bath full of hot water. He slid into it and started to wash with the soap he found in a little tiled cave at one side. The bath was so big that when he had finished washing he swam gently up and down until he felt the hot water too enervating and climbed out. The two men immediately wrapped him in towels, and led him to a chair, where he sat down while one of them shaved him and the other manicured his nails.

When they had finished Christopher dressed again and tried to get an answer out of the men. They stood for a

127

few seconds looking as though they had not understood what he was saying, and then, in unison, opened wide their mouths. Christopher felt that there was something wrong with these mouths, but it was a moment or two before he realized that neither man had a tongue.

He felt that he had wandered into some tale out of an oriental book and was being attended to by speechless eunuchs. The linnet, they said, sang better if its tongue were split with a silver coin, but these men had had their tongues cauterized at the root. He saw that the men had gone beyond the reach of words, and that any offer of sympathy would be like a word of kindness to a starving man. All that was left to them was death, and he was not judge to offer that.

He was led back along the corridor and up the marble stairway into a large room where Omar Junior and the captain were waiting.

"Let's go and have a bit of lunch," Omar Junior said as he entered, and they went through a doorway at the back of the room, into a large hall with a huge table, set for six people.

No sooner were they seated than a woman advanced from the far end and took her seat beside Omar Junior. She was followed by two others, who took their place beside Christopher and the captain.

Then the prisoners who acted as servants started bringing in the lunch. It was a very curious meal, Christopher thought, full of the richest and most extraordinary dishes; a whole peacock, a sturgeon, and a platter full of lark's tongues were among the delicacies offered.

As if reading his thoughts, Omar Junior remarked, "This lunch you are now eating is a replica of one that was once served to an Emperor. What do you think of the wine? It's genuine falernian, I can assure you. I don't consider it bad at this date and in this time to be able to serve a meal like this.

128

At the end of lunch they were entertained by a conjuror; a very childish entertainment Christopher thought, with tricks which seemed to consist for the most part of bringing naked girls out of hats and walking-sticks. As the conjuror produced these girls from different objects in the room, they fell in in a row and stood at attention until he had finished. Then they burst into a frenzy of dancing, to the music that came from a large radio-gramophone set in one side of the sideboard that ran nearly the whole length of the room.

The prisoners kept on filling the wine glasses, with the result that Christopher quickly became rather drunk, and started embracing the woman beside him, speaking endearments that he did not mean. He noticed, during a pause between kisses, that the captain was doing the same, but that Omar Junior was nearly hidden under the heap of girls who were playing some game with him.

After that Christopher could remember little. He had a rough impression of drinking a great deal more and of dancing madly round the room. He seemed to be seeing nothing but the naked bodies of women in all sorts of positions, with, occasionally, the face of Omar or of his son grinning up between a pair of legs. He remembered very clearly sitting down to eat again and rising suddenly to his feet as if to make a speech, but instead of speaking he had been sick right across the table. This had not appeared to irritate Omar Junior in the least; he had been sitting on the table with one arm round a pretty boy who had appeared from nowhere, and the other round one of the girls. He had just burst into laughter, and had ordered the prisoner who was serving to refill Christopher's glass.

The end of the evening had come when he had found himself lying on a pile of cushions which threatened to smother him if he moved, so that he had been forced to lie still while one of the women had tried to give him a drink by filling her mouth with wine and squirting it through his lips.

CHAPTER TEN

WHEN he woke in the morning Christopher found himself lying in a huge bed in the middle of an otherwise empty room. He was alone. He rose gingerly and realized that someone had undressed him and that his clothes were lying in a neat heap at the foot of the bed. He felt very ill, and walked towards the door to try and find a cold tap where he could wash his head to clear his fumed brain.

Outside the door two of the prisoners were standing. They took his arms and led him along to another room, somewhat like the one where he had bathed the previous day. There they shoved him into a Turkish-bath where he was nearly scalded and then into a cold bath, where he was forced to remain steady because one of them started to shave him. After that they gave him a massage, pummelling him till he felt that his muscles would never again respond to his reflexes. In the end, however, he was forced to admit to himself that he certainly did feel better than when he had crawled out of bed. The men led him back to his room where he sat on the edge of the bed, dressing slowly.

A knock at the door roused him, and he called to the knocker to enter. It was the captain, looking slightly drawn about the corners of his nose and with faint pencillings under his eyes. "God!" he said, "that was a beezer and no mistake. I still feel half-tight. Juney's a wonderful chap, you know, been up and about for the last two hours, and done nearly all his day's work. He never has a hangover, he says, and I believe him. I've been with him on a blind that lasted three days, and he was still as fresh as a daisy at the end. How do you feel?"

"Not too bad now, thanks. What happened to me last night? I got most frightfully tight, didn't I?"

"By God, yes, you were funny! You should have seen your face just after you'd been sick across the table. You were pale green, and your eyes looked as though they were going to drop out of your head."

Suddenly the captain seemed to recollect that Christopher was not an old school friend who had been out on the spree with him, but merely his prisoner. He straightened up, clicking his heels smartly, and said, "Well, Christopher, I suppose we'd better have a spot of breakfast now. After that I expect Juney will tell you what's to happen. I'm awfully sorry and all that, old chap, but you know, orders are orders and so on, and even Juney needs to obey his old man. His governor would have no hesitation in ordering his son's degradation and even his execution if he heard he'd crossed him."

They went along another corridor, another lateral burrow in the warren, to a small room with subdued lighting, where they had a light breakfast of grape-fruit, rolls and coffee. Then the captain took Christopher from the house and led him across the square at the back, to a squat square of white concrete, relieved only by two forbidding black windows through which nothing could be seen.

The man in the blue silk uniform came up on his tractor with its mounted machine-gun trained on them, but stopped short on recognizing the captain, saluting smartly before he turned away. Christopher and the captain came to a door in the side of the building, which the latter opened by twirling a combination lock until the tumblers fell.

The whole of the room they entered seemed to be

occupied by an enormous desk, covered with neat piles of papers. At the far side, a spider in the middle of its web, Omar Junior sat grinning at them. He beckoned them to come to his side, laying down the book he was reading. With considerable difficulty they squeezed in beside the desk. Christopher glanced at the book and noted that it dealt with the sexual life of the ancient Persians, illustrated with anatomical distortions and exaggerations by some modern hand.

"Ah, ha! And how are we this morning, Rolfe, eh?" Omar Junior began, his voice heavy with joviality. "Feeling a bit under the weather, what? Ah, that's bad —very bad—shouldn't feel like that you know. Ah, yes, Christopher, I suppose you've heard your sentence? Yes? Well, then you won't want me to repeat it? I don't know what's come over the old man these days. Probably G.P.I.—next thing we'll hear is that he's taken up fighting with his furniture, or is sentencing his carpet to fly around his room whenever he enters it. This is the second recent occasion on which he has let his sense of humour run away with him. You remember the last one, Rolfe—I think you acted as escort? The chap who had to collect ten million cowries? You know he was a harmless enough chap, and when he turned up one day and announced that he'd finished his task, I thought it quite probable that he had found a hoard somewhere. So I sent out two of my best warders with him and a boy to bring back a message if they wanted carriers. Well, the boy came back about three hours later, soaked to the skin, to shiver out his story. Apparently the chap had led them into a cave and delayed them there till the tide turned and trapped them. The boy escaped by being thin enough to squeeze out between two rocks, but the others were drowned. I went down myself the next day, before writing my report, and saw the bodies all right, but there wasn't a single cowrie. Apparently the chap had spent his time just

132

sitting there thinking how to commit suicide and take someone with him. The funny thing about it, which makes me think the old man's going a bit queer, is that his reply to my report regretted the fact that the man had not collected the cowries, as he needed them very badly. What he wanted them for, God only knows—I don't. Anyhow, I hope, Christopher, that you're not contemplating something of the same sort, for I can't afford to lose any more men."

Christopher assured him that he was not, as yet, thinking of committing suicide. He hoped that the equipment he would receive would be decent, as it would load the dice against him to neglect to supply him with charts and other necessities, and he presumed that Omar had not intended the sentence to be capital.

"Oh, that's all being attended to just now," Omar replied, with what Christopher thought was a decidedly unpleasant laugh. "You'll get the best we have here. No charts though, I'm sorry, for you're still a technical prisoner, and we can hardly hand you the means of escape. You can start now, or if you'd rather, you can wait till after lunch. I'm having rather a pleasant meal to-day—the exact replica of a nineteenth-century feast, with all the correct pauses for being sick, and so on."

Christopher shuddered at the thought of another orgy like the one he had been party to the previous day, and politely declined the invitation to lunch, saying that he would like to make a start as soon as possible, as he wished to travel a good distance before nightfall. However, he would be delighted to accept an invitation to lunch on his return, should one be offered to him.

Omar Junior bowed and said he would be honoured if Mr. Aukland would deign to grace his poor table with his presence at the successful conclusion of his present venture. Christopher had a feeling that they were all in a play, and that this politeness, and the bowing and scraping that went with it, was a part of the stage directions. Backed up by the disciplined correctitude of the captain, he and Omar kept the farce alive until they reached the edge of the cliff beyond the Penal Settlement.

He did not feel a prisoner any longer, but, rather, an explorer just about to set out on a perilous voyage. Almost without realizing it, he was bowing to the invisible crowd who edged his path, throwing invisible caps into the air, and shouting soundless cheers.

For a few minutes he was the hero, the man going out into the unknown to face unimagined dangers to bring back the fabled but remembered phœnix. He knew that he was walking slightly more upright than usually, and that there was a swagger in his step that was quite foreign to his usual stumbling gait, but, after all, one must allow the hero some self-consciousness before the eyes, admiring and adoring, of the men and women who surrounded him.

He felt that the Great Auk was as good as captured, for what could withstand the fury of his course. For himself there was no reason for the expedition, save only that of doing what was expected of him by his devoted followers and worshippers.

Omar Junior was his manager, the small star to whom some glory yet accrues from its connexion with the major star, the largest in the constellation.

They entered a small porcelain-lined lift at the top of the cliff, and, as Omar Junior pressed a button and they shot rapidly down the shaft, all Christopher's illusions were left behind, to be blown away by the stiff wind that whipped the harsh grass back from the verge of the cliff. The journey downward was long, but as last the lift slowed and eased gradually to a stop.

Leaving through the sliding doors, Christopher saw that they were on a rocky beach, and that, on either side of the lift-shaft, gangs of prisoners were working, hewing the great blocks of granite from the face of the cliff with bleeding fingers and torn nails, nails worn to the quick by the rub of rock that glittered so cheerfully with fragments of mica. These prisoners were guarded by warders, each carrying a thin, sharp whip, and there was not one who did not bear the marks of the cruel lash across his exposed shoulders.

The godlike indifference of Omar Junior to these poor wretches angered Christopher, but he did not dare to speak his mind, as he had no knowledge of the boundaries of power and was afraid that he, too, might be set to quarry with the others.

As they walked away from the working party, Christopher hoped that if ever he did return it would be to find that a revolution had taken place, and that these slaves of the State had been freed.

"What do you do with the blocks of granite when you've got them cut to shape?" he asked.

"Do with them? What do you mean—why should we do anything with them? We throw them into the sea," Omar replied. "However, I'll admit we do make some use of the chips that the masons discard. We use them in making concrete."

"Isn't it a frightful waste to set all these wretches to cut blocks of stone and not use the results of their labour for something really worth while?"

"Not in the least. I can see, my dear chap, that you don't know or understand much about the punishment of criminals. Why, if we started using the results of their labour they might begin to think that they were indispensable, and that would never do with fellows like these. Of course, in some places, where the criminals are not really serious offenders like these, we do set them to do useful work, such as digging clay and making moulds for fancy bricks. But here we just cut granite, or make salt,

135

and throw them back into the sea. As a matter of fact, neither the granite nor the salt are of a good enough quality to be worth using. That may explain a lot, but it does not alter the principle of the thing."

Christopher nodded wisely as if he understood exactly what Omar Junior meant, and they continued down the shore towards a rocky point. In this strange existence, he noticed, the sea at least smelled as it always did, the fishy odour of decaying seaweed mingled with the scent of iodine from the same source.

As they walked Christopher kicked the thick rhubarby sticks of wrack. He was the village idiot being taken for a walk by two kind gentlemen, who had to agree with everything they said, or else they might withhold the usual present at the finish of his outing, the handful of caramels or the cheap packet of cigarettes. His eyes goggled inanely at the sight of the salmon-pink starfish and the many-fingered anemones in the pools. He was a good boy and good boys always got their just reward; perhaps, if he was awfully good and they felt terribly kind, one of the gentlemen would give him a nice bright new silver penny.

It was fun to kick little bits off the rocks so that they went splash into the pools, but that was bad for his boots, and he was not yet due to be issued with another pair. The pyrites glittered in the slaty rock in one place, and it was with considerable difficulty that Christopher restrained himself from falling on all fours and trying to pull it out. But of course he could not do it with these people beside him; it was his private gold-mine, and when he came back he would make a fortune out of it. He was lucky to find a gold-mine just like that; it went to show the value of observation. Here these men had been passing the place every day, and they had not even noticed the bright and shining outcrop.

He was going to be sent away, he knew, but when he

came back he would be a great man and they would be proud to know him. They would shake his hand and say, "Well done, Christopher, we never thought you'd manage it." Then he would be given a feast, and he would have lovely things to eat, and they might even make him a king. He was a lucky boy.

The sound of Omar Junior's voice suddenly made him recollect where he was, and what was about to take place. "We're nearly there now, my dear boy," the sleek Persian-cat voice was saying. "I'm afraid that when I said I'd see that you got the best equipment that we could give you it didn't mean very much. You'll understand that it's against our policy to have too many boats about here —the prisoners might take it into their heads to escape from our benevolent care. But I do hope that you'll believe me when I say that this really is the best we can give you."

They came to a ridge of rock, topped with short hard grass and round cushions of sea-pink, and went over it. A few feet below them Christopher could see a small boat, about seventeen feet in length, with the mast ready stepped up. She did not appear to be the right sort of boat for a rough sea, as her beam was as narrow as a needle in proportion to her length.

"I say," he exclaimed, "that's a boat that's meant to stick pretty close to the coast line, not one for the open sea. It's practically suicide to risk a squall in her."

"I'm afraid it's the best we can do for you," he was told, "and we've tried to fit her up as well as possible. Just to make you feel more at home I've given her a familiar name. That'll cheer you up, eh?"

Christopher looked at the stern and there, carefully carved and picked out in silver letters, he read the name *MALI*. "My God," he said, "that's a pretty good joke, isn't it?" He burst into hysterical laughter and was forced

137

to sit down on the rocks. Omar Junior and the captain looked at him in astonishment, as if uncertain whether to give a few sympathetic titters or not. He wiped the tears from his eyes with his leather sleeve.

"It's really not too bad a boat," Omar Junior cajoled, "and I'm sure you'll grow to like her. After all, if we had managed to get you a bigger boat, you'd have found her difficult to manage all by yourself."

He went on speaking, but Christopher was not listening to him. He had just realized that he was to be completely alone on his venture. Before he had thought about it, but the fact of his loneliness had never sunk in. He had assumed that he would be accompanied by escorting bands of angels or dolphins or something of the kind.

He climbed down the edge of the rocks into the boat and waved up to Omar Junior and the captain, shouting, "I'll go now. Good-bye." He untied the rope that held the boat to a ring fixed in the rock and pushed her off. He thought he would not hoist his sail until he got clear of the rocks, and, taking a long pole which lay on the rock, started punting his way out of the narrow bay.

Fortunately the sea was calm beyond the point, and he let the boat lie a few feet from the rock, fending her off every now and again. He heard Omar Junior shouting, and looked up to see him stumbling among the rocks, hurrying out to the point, followed in a more leisurely manner by the captain.

"Look here, old man," Omar Junior panted when he was only a few feet from the boat, "you were in such a hell of a hurry to get going that I damn near forgot to give you this. It's a sort of compass dingus which will guide you back to here once you've bagged your Great Auks. The old man told me to give you it, but to tell you that if you came back without the birds you'd be executed on the spot. Sorry to give you this as a parting message, but that's what I was told to do."

He threw a small object into the cockpit, and Christopher picked it up, noticing that it was a small compass, but that the luminous dot did not point towards the direction which he knew to hold the magnetic pole, but towards the Penal Settlement. He tucked it into his pocket and repeated his good-byes. While he was raising the sail, with considerable difficulty, as all he knew about boats had come from the sea stories he had read as a child, Omar Junior continued talking: "Remember, you're to come and lunch with me when you get back," his voice the voice of a host speeding a week-end guest. "I hope you'll have decent weather. If I were you I'd go towards the north-east. There's a lot of clusters of uninhabited islands there, and your birds might be found on one of the islands. Best of luck, and don't forget my invitation."

Christopher had the sail up, and somehow, he did not know how, was moving away from the land. He turned, his hand on the tiller, bellowing, "You'd be a better man if you gave your lunches to your prisoners. How the hell would you like to have to work the whole time with a whip curling round your shoulders whenever you paused to draw a breath? Of course, you'd die of whipping in a day or two, as you're too flabby and soft to do any real work. You know where you can put your lunches—and I hope you die of constipation!"

Omar Junior did not appear to be in the least disconcerted. He clapped his knees with large soft white hands, nearly bent double with mirth. The captain said nothing, and it occurred to Christopher that he might be suffering from repression in the presence of Omar Junior, as he had hardly spoken all morning. Perhaps he was not sure how he had behaved the previous night, and was waiting to see what Omar Junior said about it, or perhaps he was just suffering from a very violent hangover.

Anyhow, now that he was away from them, Christopher

realized that the relationship between them was none of his business, and it looked as though he was going to be fully occupied in managing his boat. He tried to tidy up the sail, which sagged and bulged in the most unaccountable places.

Once he had set the sail to right he found that there was a gadget for fixing the tiller, and he fastened it with the boat's bows pointing towards the north-east, thanking his lucky stars for the favourable wind, as he was not sure about the business of tacking against the wind. He opened the hatch and entered the tiny cabin.

He found it was pretty well fitted up, with a paraffin stove, decent rugs on the bunk, a cork jacket, fishing lines, various tins of food, and a small but powerful-looking air-rifle. He looked at this last object for a moment, wishing that he had known it was there earlier, as it would have added point to his outburst at Omar Junior, if only he had been able to pot the fat slob in the belly with a slug.

The boat seemed to be wobbling in the most peculiar fashion, so he left the cabin to find that, somehow, the sails were just flapping, and the boat itself was just bobbing up and down on the waves without moving at all. He decided that even if he was not getting anywhere he was in no danger, and so he returned to the cabin, where he ate sardines from one tin spread on bread taken from another.

Then he made up his mind that he would make a new start. This took him a few minutes, as every time he thought he had managed to get going the tiller took the boat out of the wind, leaving him rolling about as before. Eventually he did manage to make a start, and then he remembered that he had seen a book on sailing small boats in the cabin. He risked diving back to get it.

Though this took him less than half a minute the boat

had lost the wind again, and was yawing about like a bit of driftwood. This time he seemed to have discovered the knack, for after one failure he set off towards the north. Holding the tiller in one hand, he balanced the book in the other. It was full of technical phrases, so he found that he could understand little of it. After reading right through it without understanding much, he became exasperated and pitched it overboard, to watch it bobbing away behind him.

Once it was out of sight he wished he had not been so hasty, as the book might have proved useful. Surely, if he had looked at it hard enough and carefully enough, he would have been able to puzzle out the nautical terms and change them into a simpler phraseology. However, as they said, it was no use crying over spilt milk or over books which were feeding the fishes.

He kept his eyes ahead of him, hoping that there were no sharp hidden rocks in his path, waiting to tear the bottom out of the boat. He wished he had been given a chart, even if it had only been one of the coast-line. However, if he could manage to live and was not drowned, he would be free of the Omar family for as long as he liked, which certainly was something to be thankful for.

It occurred to him that it would be quite a good idea to try and catch some fish, even though he had not the slightest idea of how to do it, and, this time not minding whether the boat did lose the wind or not, he returned to the cabin and looked through the fishing tackle. There were glass jars full of bait, silver sand eel and pallid prawn, but he decided to try his luck with a line to which some flies were attached. They were not at all the sort of flies to which he was accustomed, the miniature silk-bodied spiders, gnats and mayflies of the trout fisherman, or tinsel and peacock's and pheasant's feather doctors of the man who sought the salmon. These flies were tied roughly on common tinned hooks, and merely consisted of a bit of a gull's feather, dyed or plain, with a rough body of twisted wool.

Obviously the salt water fish, if they were attracted by these flies, which Christopher did not expect, were less fastidious than those of mountain burn or downland stream. There was no rod for him to cast the flies with, so he unwound a few yards of line and threw it over the stern, paying out till the flies were skipping along the surface of the water about twenty yards behind him.

As he had expected, the fish did not seem to relish these most untempting flies. However, as he had let them out, he thought he might as well let them remain. With one hand on the tiller and the other fingering the line, he went towards the blank horizon that, perhaps, was not as blank as he had thought it—were there not one or two little lumps protruding from the sea towards the north-east?

He strained his eyes towards these spots, and gradually edged the boat round until her bows were aimed at them. He looked back at the land he had left, and was surprised to find that he was quite a long way from the shore. He could no longer distinguish the figures that he knew were working on the beach, and, as a matter of fact, he was not quite sure that he was looking at the right place, for there seemed to be several white outcrops along the coast, and any one of them might have been the Penal Settlement.

The sea was not as smooth as it had been near the land, and Christopher felt slightly ill. He assured himself that he was not about to be sea-sick, but was forced to admit that he did not feel any too well. His eyes felt rather too large for his face, and his tongue had become sticky and slightly too fat. It would never do for him to give way to sea-sickness, for in addition to manning the boat, he had to keep a sharp look-out for a Great Auk.

He fixed his eyes firmly on the bronze end of the tiller,

and tried to tell himself that he had never felt better in all his life, and that he would quickly bring his task to a successful conclusion. However, he allowed that he really did not feel very interested in anything at all. If a pink whale with purple spots had spouted just beside the boat, addressing him by name, he would have waved it away with a bored and listless hand.

Just as he was beginning to feel that he certainly would be sick, something happened which made him forget all about it. The line he was holding began to jerk in his hand. He had a bite. He was not sure of the correct procedure with sea-fish, whether to pull it straight in or play it like a trout, but the thickness of the line led him to think that the former was probably the correct course.

Carefully, keeping it taut all the time, Christopher started to wind in the line on to the wooden square which acted as a reel. When the flies came within sight of the boat, he was astonished to see that he had not caught one fish but three, one on each of the flies. Standing up, he tried to swing the fish into his boat, but only managed to get two of them on board, for the third struck the side and fell off the hook back into the sea.

Christopher unhooked his catch, which he recognized as mackerel, and threw the line back in the wake of the boat. It barely seemed to touch the water before the flies were grabbed by other eager fish. For about ten minutes they bit furiously, but then, though the line dragged behind the boat invitingly the flies appeared as unattractive as a beefsteak in a vegetarian restaurant.

He had caught twenty-three fish, and tried to remember, from the days he had spent trout-fishing as a child, how he should set about cleaning them, for he knew that it was not good to leave the guts in for long. He fetched a sharp knife from the cabin and, first killing the fish by knocking their heads sharply on the edge of the cockpit, he slit them up the belly and removed their guts, yellow coiled bags like lug-worms, and threw them overboard.

Although he would have been willing to swear that there was not a gull in sight a minute before he started his gutting operations, Christopher, when he raised his eyes, saw gulls gathering from all directions for the feast, dipping at the guts before they reached the water, and screaming when another's neat sideslip robbed them of the dainty which they had set their eyes upon.

When he had finished cleaning the fish Christopher wondered how he was to keep them at all fresh, for he did not seem to have salt enough to cover them with it. He threaded a piece of string through their gaping gills and let them dangle in the sea, hoping the brine was strong enough to keep them edible.

It occurred to him that he was being rather greedy in keeping his fishing-line out after he had made so good a catch, and he wound it in, rather shamefacedly, as if afraid he was being watched by an adverse critic.

The smudges on the horizon were now clearer, and Christopher could see that they were indeed islands. A cluster of rocks where the waves broke white and the spray seemed to make innumerable little rainbows during the instant it hung in the air.

It did not look as though it was going to be any too easy to find a place to anchor his boat, but he went on towards the islands, having completely forgotten the impulse he had had to be sick. The islands were not so far away as he had at first thought, and as he approached he supposed the misty spray which surrounded them must have given them the appearance of being hidden on the horizon.

The sea was still rather rough, but the little boat, for he would not call her *The Mali*, heeled at an angle and rode easily over the waves, and a stiff breeze carried him steadily towards his objective. It looked as though there

144

might be hidden reefs round the islands, but he would just have to risk that, as he had no method of plotting the way ahead of him.

He felt fairly cheerful in spite of his hopeless undertaking. When he was within half a mile of the islands he noticed that there was a gap between two of the most terrifying, and the sea inside seemed to be as smooth as the sea of the bay from which he had set out. He turned his bows towards the gap, and before he was ready for it, found himself shooting through the opening, borne on a strong current. Several times he seemed about to hit some sharp spur of black rock which stuck threateningly up in the water, and tried to make use of his tiller to turn away, but always the current was stronger than he was and carried him past in safety.

When at last the rush of water carried the boat into a calm bay, walled with islands which bore the brunt of the sea's attack, Christopher's scalp felt as though it had shrunk and was bursting over his skull, and cold drops of sweat coursed down his temples.

He edged the boat into a sheltered corner and furled the sails as neatly as he could. Up in the bows he found a light anchor and dropped it overboard, hoping that there was enough rope attached to it.

The anchor did not run out far, and when he gave the rope a steady pull he found that the flukes had bitten in the rocky bottom, and he was quite secure. He went into the cabin and brought out the paraffin stove, thinking it wise to keep the air in the cabin pure for as long as possible. He cooked two of his afternoon's captures. To-morrow morning he would look around the rocks, seeking traces of the mythical Great Auk.

CHAPTER ELEVEN

THE soft rippling of the waves against his cabin woke
Christopher. He was heavy-eyed and dull brained, but
pulled himself out of the bunk and went out into the
cockpit. The sun shone palely over a very blue sea. He
supposed it would be good for him to take a dip, and
stood naked for a moment or two testing the water. It
was very cold indeed, and he decided that he would not
go in after all, but being unused to balancing on a boat,
he tilted her over and was flung into the water.

Once he was in, it was not so bad. He swam over to
one of the little rocks that lined his lagoon, and scrambled
ashore, scraping his knees on the barnacles that covered
the rock below high-water mark.

The rocks were whitened with the droppings of sea
birds, long silver stains across the black. A tern swung
swiftly past his head, and a glowing white plummet, a
gannet, plunged in the waters, but he saw no signs of the
bird he sought.

He swam round the other islands, but with no better luck.
He saw all sorts of sea birds, the ungainly guillemot, the
black-backed gull, skuas, petrels, and even, peeping from
a rabbit hole on one of the larger islands which was crowned
with grass, the chunky blue and orange beak of a puffin.

Back on his boat, Christopher made himself breakfast
and then started to puzzle out his way of exit from the
lagoon; the tide seemed to be rising and would shortly
be full. There was the barest fringe of seaweed visible on
the rocks, and it occurred to him that, having come in
on the flow the previous night, he would now need to
make use of the ebb to carry him forth.

146

Raising the anchor was not easy, for it stuck firmly and dragged but refused to leave the rocky bottom. Christopher tried pulling the boat first one way and then the other, and, eventually, feeling its weight as though it was made of lead or was as large as the anchor of a battleship, he pulled it slowly up to him, remembering to coil the rope neatly as it came on board to obviate a tangle later. It was little wonder that the anchor felt heavy, for the bend was festooned with a parcel of various weeds, and across the flukes a ribbon of weed had bound a large water-logged piece of wood, the remnant of some shipwreck.

Christopher went gingerly towards the channel, keeping his sails furled and pushing his way along the rocks with the long pole. As he entered the channel the under-current took hold of the boat and he no longer needed to push his way along with the pole, but rather had to use it as a brake to slow down his progress. He was not very good at this job, and the boat began to turn, at first slowly, but gathering speed fast, until, as he entered the channel proper, the little boat was spinning like a small boy's top under the impact of his whip.

It was fortunate that he had tried to get out at full tide, for several times he felt the keel scrape, ever so gently, on some hidden rock, and he knew that if he had hit one of these reefs fair and square at the pace he was travelling, the bottom would have been torn from the boat. It made him feel quite sick to find himself buzzing round like a dervish, and the sight of the sharp spikes that loomed on either side of him was not comforting. It was no use trying to do anything, for if he had put out the pole the force of the water combined with his speed would have torn it from his grasp.

Although the channel was not long, it seemed to Christopher that they took hours to pass through it, now spinning near one black wall and now near the other, with the keel scraping and jarring fitfully over rocky bars. At length, however, they were free of the enclosing walls, and, although the boat kept turning in circles for a little while, Christopher was able to assure himself that, somehow, more by good luck than good guidance, they were safe.

Slowly, as if every movement hurt him, he unfurled the sail, pulling the cord that raised it to the top of the mast. There was a stiffish breeze blowing as he turned north, and the little boat heeled over so that the water whisked briskly along the deck, just a few inches from Christopher. He did not feel that this was a very safe method of progression, and wished he knew how to slow the boat down. There were, he believed, things called reefs, and you took them in, but he was afraid to touch the strings on the sail which apparently were those reefs, as he was afraid he might upset the boat if he started moving about.

So he sat as still as he could in the cockpit, merely moving the tiller enough to keep the boat's head turned towards the north. He did not dare to fix the line which was fixed to a corner of the sail, but held it firmly in the hand that he did not need for the tiller, ready to let it go if he thought he was in danger.

After a while Christopher found that he was not really frightened at all, and that he was rather enjoying the sensation of skipping along on top of the waves like one of the flat stones that boys threw on to the canals to see how many jumps they could make. He kept his eyes fixed ahead of him on the water, on the watch for submerged reefs.

He was the crack yachtsman, his leather suit turned into the well-cut and neatly-creased flannels, dazzling in the sun. Holding both the tiller and the line from the sail in one hand for a moment, he felt in his pockets for his pipe, the well-polished briar with, perhaps, just the suggestion of burning round the edge of the bowl, but all he could find in his pockets was a packet of cigarettes, and he recalled that he did not smoke a pipe.

This, however, did not disturb his fantasy, for he lit a cigarette and cocked it perkily in the corner of his mouth. Now he was the gentleman adventurer out of fiction. The suave debonair hero who always smoked like that, and who was insolent to those who tried to order him about. The smoke curved away from the glowing tip in a line like the trail from an express train, and the red end hissed gently as the flying spray hit it.

Christopher felt pleased with himself, for now he was his own master, pledged to one search only. They could not blame him if he failed, but, of course, the hero did not know a failure, but came home covered with glory and with the plaudits of the crowd ringing in his ears. He lounged easily in the cockpit, playing tricks with the tiller so that the boat tilted further over and scudded more rapidly across the expanse of water.

His escape lay northwards, and as none knew that north he might manage to finish his quest quickly; perhaps he would encounter a colony of Gair Fowl on some forgotten island, some bare rock that had not been considered worthy of the sailor's investigation.

When he felt hungry he worked gently with the tiller until he had taken the boat out of the wind, and then, running no risks, for the hero was always careful despite his devil-may-care appearance, he furled the sails and, going into the cabin, cooked himself a meal. He was pleased to note that they had remembered he would need much water, and he examined his two large tanks with interest, and fingered an arrangement of tubes and kettles which could be used to make drinking water from the sea.

After lunch he tied the reefs round the boom, tidily tucking away loose ends, as he unfurled the sails. There seemed to be very little sail left, but Christopher found that there was quite enough to carry him along at a fair speed and yet leave the boat in a slightly more upright position than before. Looking at the position of the sun, he judged it to be nearly afternoon, and stared ahead anxiously, hoping for smudges on the horizon like those of the previous afternoon.

But, look as he could, straining his eyes till they felt that they were made of red-hot steel and would burn right through his soft and malleable skull, he could see nothing except the occasional splash of a gannet dropped from the sky, and the glistening backs of a school of porpoises, black and oily, snaking up and down. The only sounds were the wash of the sea, the bursting gasps of the porpoises and the shrieks of gulls. He tried to shoot at the porpoises as he drew near to them, but the slugs from his rifle merely hit the water with a smack and then ricochetted off, twanging and singing.

At nightfall he was no nearer to any sheltered spot, and, rather hopelessly, he let his anchor down to the full extent of the rope, finding no bottom and no grip for it. He let it remain in the water, however, thinking that it might hinder the drift of the boat, and turned in.

As he lay, half asleep, he listened to the waves washing against the side of the boat, and they seemed to be repeating, "You're lost, lost, lost! You're lost, lost, lost!" He was unwilling to admit, even to himself, that he did not know where he was, and turning over so that the bedclothes covered his ears, he fell asleep.

When he went on deck in the morning he found the boat rocking gently, and that the stiff regular breeze had dropped to alternate periods of gust and calmness.

Having no landmarks, he was quite unable to tell how far the boat had drifted during the night, and he just had to hope that he had not travelled back too far, and make towards the north again. He let out the reefs he had taken in the previous day, and even with a full sail found it difficult to make steady progress.

The squalls that came lashing over the water so that he could see their approach frightened him until he found that he could overcome them by turning the boat's head towards them. He saw fish once or twice, but he could not be bothered letting out a line to try and catch them.

He sailed all day without any incident except sudden squalls and occasional showers of rain. The next day was misty, and there was little wind, so that the boat crawled like a water-beetle across the surface of the sea. The mist magnified things out of all proportion so that a piece of drifting wrack loomed beside him like an island, and a dead seagull that floated alongside appeared like a drowned sailor, the embodiment of all lost mariners risen from Davy Jones's locker.

Christopher was bored and drowsed most of the time, to startle suddenly into wakefulness at the sound of the rippling water, which had become magnified into the roar of breakers crashing on a granite coast. The sea itself was thick and heavy, and bubbles shone on the surface in many colours, like those on a pool where petrol has been spilled.

On the fifth day, however, he left his cabin to see, only a few miles ahead, a large island, with other islands behind it stretching right to the horizon. He hoisted the sail and slowly, for the wind was not much stronger than it had been the previous day, made his way towards it, edging the breeze to catch as much of it as he could. The island, though he called it large, could not have been much more than four or five acres in extent, but it was covered with grass and gorse.

On the eastern side there was a little bay which formed a break of white glaring sand, relieving the matt black of the rocks that rose to a plateau above. Christopher steered the boat into this bay, getting as near to the shore as he could before letting down his anchor. He stripped and, tying his clothes in a tight bundle, which he fastened to his head, slipped into the water, when a few leisurely strokes carried him ashore.

It felt good to place his feet on the sand, and he ran up and down the little bay once or twice before he put on his clothes again. He climbed up a steep gully at the back of the bay and stood on the firm hard turf, kicking little holes in it with his heel while he looked around.

The grass was covered with the little yellow and red flower, like a pea, which he knew as ham-and-eggs, gaunt stalks of ragwort stuck up in patches, and he noticed a stone with a pile of broken snails' shells round it, a thrush's anvil. Even then, he heard a thrush give an indignant startled cry from a clump of gorse, and felt that, for a few minutes at least, he was free of the ocean and back in the countryside where everything had its purpose, and the sloppy mess of green water had not importance, as reality or as symbol.

For a little while he lay on the short grass, breathing in the air that was so different from that of the last five days, and then he remembered the object of his landing, and went towards the highest part of the rocky cliff, where he looked over as inobtrusively as he could, in case one of the forgotten birds should be sitting on a sea-washed stone at the foot.

He saw nothing but a few gulls and a rabbit sunning itself on a ledge far beneath him. He decided to climb down the cliff, and to go round the island as near the water as he could. Step by step, with the rock crumbling beneath his boots and breaking off under the grip of his hands, he descended.

On the north side of the island he found another little bay with a stream running down over the rocks and across the sand. He went as high as he could and caught up some water in his cupped hands, grateful for its fresh-ness after the mildly brackish taste of the water on the boat. The stream running over the sand had dug a channel where flat stones and shells had gathered. Christopher sat beside it washing his feet, looking at the rosy pinkness of the quartz and the delicate fragility of the razor shells and clams that lifted slightly as the water flowed over and around them.

Down where the stream reached the sea he saw several little flounders, no bigger than pennies. They seemed to be playing a game with him, for they would lie still, practically invisible, until his hand was just about to close on them, when, with a quick flick of the tail, they would dart away.

Christopher pulled his wandering thoughts together and made his way back to the boat. When he came within sight of her he found that the tide had ebbed and she was lying tilted over on her side on the dry side. He fixed the anchor a little more firmly and took his air-rifle and climbed the hill again, determined to shoot a rabbit for his supper.

However, the only rabbit he saw did not seem to be the least frightened of him, and he did not have the heart to shoot it as it stood waiting for him to approach. He tried to scare it away by shouting, but it only ran a few feet and then stopped again, like a child playing tig. When he returned to his boat, finding her afloat again, he had a meal of boiled mackerel.

The next morning, as he put to sea, the weather looked very threatening, but the other islands did not seem to be so very far away, and he hoped to reach one of them before any storm arose. The wind was strong and gusty, and, to be on the safe side, he took in the reefs in his sail, steering as carefully as he could so that the boat should not encounter the full force of the wind.

The islands were further away than he had thought them

153

to be, and all the time the sky became darker and darker. The wind grew stronger and the little boat started to labour, attempting to wrench the tiller out of his hand. The first island, fringed by a shower of spray which showed up the hidden rocks as it fell, offered no shelter whatever, and Christopher began to feel rather frightened.

He was all alone in this boat, this cockleshell, and a storm was rising, and he did not know how to set about receiving it. He took down the sail thinking that that would make the boat a smaller target for the wind and sea, but he had to hoist it again quickly when he saw that he was driving fast towards the reefs outside the island. He remembered having read that it was good to put oil on a rough sea, but he had not enough oil to use, and so his best plan seemed to be to try and run with the storm until he reached the shelter he sought.

The boat was travelling very fast indeed, and Christopher found that it took all his strength to keep her on the course he had adopted.

Now it was all he could do to see any distance ahead of him, for the waves were taller than his masthead. He sometimes rose with one of them, and seemed to be on the top of a swing, waiting for the rope to break, but then the boat slid down into a hollow of the waves and wallowed there for a moment before starting on another climb.

He was terrified in case a wave broke suddenly, leaving the boat on top, as he was sure that she would break in two in falling from such a height. It was no longer any good trying to steer. He was not strong enough to hold the tiller, and it was wrenched free from his hand, swinging to and fro like a flail, catching him several stinging blows as he grabbed at it.

Suddenly, as quickly as it had risen, the sea was calm again, smooth as the sea on a backdrop in a theatre. The wind, however, had not slackened in the least, and

154

the boat was still tearing along, heeling now this way and now that.

Then, swimming strongly alongside in the oily water, he saw the Great Auk. He dashed into the cabin and snatched up the rifle, making the boat tilt dangerously as he did so. He saw that the bird was making for a little rock, and raised his rifle to his shoulder and pulled the trigger. He missed.

At that moment the boat bucked like a horse, and Christopher was thrown over and lost his balance. Trying to save himself, he dropped the rifle overboard. Making a grab at it without thinking, he fell over himself. As he hit the water he saw the bird rise with a frightened swish of wings, and knew that it was only a razorbill and not the object of his quest.

He seemed to go down for miles, and in spite of pushing down with feet and hands as hard as he could, it was a moment or two before he broke the surface. He shook the water from his eyes and raised himself out of the water to find the boat.

She was sailing fast, heeling right over, and as steadily as if he had been holding the tiller in a firm hand, headed towards the ugly squat black rock. Christopher realized that he would have to catch up very quickly and, putting his head down in the water, he crawled after her. He could not raise his head to take a look, as that would waste a second or two, and it seemed that even a half second might be valuable in his race.

The boat was travelling much faster than he could. She hit the half-submerged rock with a resounding crash that pulled Christopher out of his crawl in time to see her sliding back to disappear under the water.

For a moment or two he could not take in the disaster and swam on, with a leisurely breast stroke, until he reached the rock. He scrambled up the slippery surface

155

and clung there for a few seconds before the strong swirl of the ground swell carried him off.

Treading water, he tried to think what he could do. He could not, obviously, continue his search for the Great Auk without a boat. He felt quite clear-headed, and was more perturbed by the end of his quest than by the loss of his boat. That seemed to be a trifling matter, one that did not really concern him.

It really was quite funny being stuck here in the sea with no prospect whatsoever of being rescued. He gurgled gently to himself at the thought, before it occurred to him that it looked as though he was certain to drown. Still treading water, he tried to fix his position, and remembered that, through the dark clouds, he had caught a glimpse of what had seemed to be an island several miles to the north. He had not taken it in properly at the time, as he had been too engrossed in managing the boat, but he was almost sure that it was there.

Thank God I am a good strong swimmer. I should be able to get near it in two or three hours. Looking up at the cloud hidden sun, he tried to decide in which direction he was facing, and set off, slowly but strongly, towards the north.

He wondered whether he should remove his boots, but decided that, as they were not very heavy, he would first see how he managed with them on, as, undoubtedly, he would have need of them on the island, and, at the moment, they would hamper him more slung round his neck.

It was quite easy to swim, in spite of the heavy swell, and for the first hour or so he felt rather pleased with the progress he was making. But after that he began to find the going much harder, and discovered, when he tried to raise himself in the water to see if he could distinguish the island, that his strength was not as great as it had been, and that the effort failed, and in its failure tired him.

The sky seemed to be getting darker again, and the swell was breaking into waves, bitter little lashes of water that seemed to remove fragments of skin from his face as they flicked it, and that left his eyes sore and inflamed.

He was not swimming so fast now, and sometimes he seemed to be losing distance rather than gaining it. He wished he had looked around the wreck of his boat and had taken a piece of driftwood, as it would have relieved him of the growing weight of his body, which felt as though it was becoming waterlogged.

He supposed that he should remove his clothes, but it did not seem to be worth the effort. He started talking to himself, counting, "One . . . two . . . three . . . strokes . . . one . . . two . . . three . . . strokes . . ." but was forced to stop, as the sharp tongues of water entered his mouth in a bitter kiss, choking him. He went down under the water, and the strain of pushing his way up to the surface did not seem to be worth the energy he would expend.

It would be so nice just to try and breathe the water as if it was air. After all, he might be able to do it; that would only be one more queer happening to add to those that had befallen him since waking in the desert.

He opened his mouth and sucked in, but instead of the salt water he had expected, he got a mouthful of air. He opened his eyes. He was back on the surface, and, wearily, with his legs dragging, he tried to swim on towards the island which, surely, could not be very far ahead of him now.

It was curious that his eyes did not seem to be so clear as they had been; they hurt now, and it was all he could do to keep them open. Of course, it was only the action of the salt water, but it was just a little bit worrying. Naturally, he could not drown, he had only been joking with himself when he had thought of it. He was able to go on for ever and ever.

At home, in a drawer mixed up with other odds and ends, he had a little silver cup. He had won it for swimming. He was the best in the school, and so he could not drown.

All the same, it was rather disturbing to find that your body did not react to your wishes as fast as it should have done. He was being forced to take rests now. To turn over on his back and let the waves bear the weight of his sagging body for a minute or two before he swam on, ever so slowly, with precise and determined strokes that showed an inclination to stir up the water instead of pulling him through it.

His mind was not working properly; there seemed to be gaps when no thoughts entered, and he was swimming mechanically, like a clockwork doll without thoughts or wishes. The sea was very rough now, and he was thrown about by the waves, one moment seeming high as the roof of a house, the next flat on the earth.

His hands were no longer functioning as he ordered them, but merely flapped foolishly beside him, helping to keep him awash. He would need to rest, and let the waves carry him along with them; perhaps they would throw him up on the shore of the island.

How long he drifted along like this he did not know. All he was aware of was that the waves were beating him about and that somehow he still breathed air. He was past caring about the blackness that would come over him and the way he would sink, his head lolling on his neck like a flower on a broken stalk.

He was dreaming now. He was being chased by men in a boat, and was swimming speedily away from them, as the razorbill had fled from him. The ease with which he swam was wonderful—just a flick of his arms gave him a vast push forward, but the men in the boat travelled even faster. They were overhauling him, and he could not fly away, for his wings had withered away and become arms. They were shouting as they made up on him, and he was straining every muscle to make his escape.

The sea was parting before him, and he was travelling like a speed boat, leaving a vast shattering wash behind him. The men in the black boat were not travelling nearly so fast—they could not be travelling so fast—they were making no splash. They were just pulling stolidly at their oars, but their doggedness seemed to be serving them better than his unexpected turn of speed did him. They were catching up. One of them, a bearded and uncouth fellow, stood in the bows, holding aloft a boat-hook.

He was barely six feet ahead now, and could travel no faster. Escape might be impossible, but at least they would not find him a docile captive.

He turned and the man in the bows hit him over the head with the boat-hook. He seemed to be falling into a black hole full of all sorts of filthy creatures, stinging jellyfish, cuttlefish, poison asps and scorpions. Then there was nothing except a slow movement, up and down, and up and down.

CHAPTER TWELVE

T HE swaying had stopped and he was lying on hard ground. He could not move at all. His eyes seemed to be crusted up with salt and his tongue filled his mouth. He heard a voice and managed to pull his eyes gradually open. The first thing he saw was the black-bearded man who had hit him over the head with the boat-hook. He was talking to two other men in a strange language, one of which Christopher was ignorant, emphasizing his remarks with angry sweeps of his hands, red and cracked from the salt water.

There was a great deal of noise all around Christopher, and he tried to concentrate on what had happened. He saw that he was in a little stone hut, and the noise he heard was the noise of a gale beating against it. It was very uncomfortable lying as he was, so Christopher tried to move into a more comfortable position. Then he realized that he was bound up in a length of cord and was completely helpless.

He tried to shout to the men to release him at once, but when he opened his mouth all that came was a strange savage croak. At the noise, however, the black-bearded man crossed the room and, standing over him, looked down and rolled him over with a push of his sea-boots. Christopher tried to explain that he wanted to be freed and that he was thirsty, but only managed to produce another series of grunts. The man, however, seemed to understand part of his request. Returning to the table, he picked up a mug of water, which he poured over Christopher's face so that he could suck up the drops that ran past his mouth.

Then the man returned to the table, and Christopher was left to croak and grunt as he liked, for no one paid the least attention as they went on with their angry argument, shouting and banging the table with clenched fists.

Christopher did not know what he could do, and after a few minutes he fell silent. He could see through the small window of thick green glass that it was dusk outside. One of the men started to trim an oil lamp. Christopher tried once more to move, but found he could not. He felt very ill. His head was full of jangling noises, and the whine and bluster of the gale seemed to grow in intensity. The three men continually glanced at the window as if afraid it would be blown in.

160

Something about their behaviour told Christopher that they were frightened of him. They kept on glancing at him from the corners of furtive eyes. He was sure he would die if they kept him tied up for much longer without food. He started croaking again to try and suggest that they undid his bonds. For a few minutes they paid no attention, but finally the bearded man muttered to his companions and rose to his feet. He stretched his arms before he crossed to Christopher. As he walked across the hut he smiled, and Christopher decided that the men had made up their minds to free him.

He stood looking down, a pink fringe of smile peering from between the black wires of his beard and moustache. Christopher gave a croak intended to express gratitude. The man drew back his foot and sent the heavy leather, copper-trimmed, sea-boot crashing against his temple.

When Christopher recovered consciousness it was again light, but the gale had not abated in the least. In fact, it seemed to be stronger, and the little stone hut seemed to be swaying slightly under the buffeting it received from every gust. His head hurt so much that it felt as though it was in two pieces, and his eyes burned as though they would sink right into his skull, like pieces of hot metal dropped on butter.

The bearded man gave him a drink and then they left him alone. He spent most of the day trying to wriggle free from his bonds, but the knots were too secure and he could not slip them. The rest of the time he passed in a sort of semi-conscious doze.

With the evening the men seemed to grow more timid than before. Christopher heard the wind howling and the rocks crashing down outside the hut, and understood that they might well be frightened. He dozed over again.

The man with the black beard was looking down at him. He formed the word "water" with his lips and, as the man paid no attention, tried to whisper it.

At the sound the man started back and his companions cowered down at the far side of the table, staring at Christopher with frightened eyes.

They stayed in a huddled bunch all night, talking in low voices. Christopher watched their every movement as he thought longingly of the cool stream where he had bathed his feet on the island.

Before daylight came the lamp burned out, and none of the men dared fetch more oil for it from the drum which stood by Christopher's head. He jerked and turned, but was still unable to loosen his bonds. Whenever he heard one of the men make a movement he cried out for water. There was immediate silence.

As the dawn began to lighten the hut, the clear dullness of a stormy day, Christopher looked over to the men and saw that their eyes were fixed in horror on the ground near his chest. There, in a little heap, lay the bronze ladybirds that he had found in the desert. The men seemed to be terrified by the sight of them. They crossed their fingers and muttered to each other until Christopher managed to roll his body over on top of the ladybirds.

All day the men remained crouching like frightened children, and with the afternoon the gale, though Christopher would not have thought it possible, seemed to practically redouble its force. The hut shook as if it was the centre of an earthquake.

The two men who had been in the background now started to argue with the black-bearded leader, seeming to try and force some line of action upon him. He seemed to disapprove of every thing they said, and shook his head solemnly so that his beard wagged like the pendulum of a clock.

Christopher started shouting at them, vast bursts of meaningless sound that hid the curses he poured down upon their frightened heads.

162

At last the black-bearded man seemed to come to a decision. He cleared his throat noisily, spat on his hands, and stood up, straightening the red cloth that was knotted round his neck. A particularly vicious gust hit the hut, and he paused for a long minute before he went slowly over to a corner behind his companions, filled with bits of wood and the other odds and ends of fishermen.

He stood beside the pile, rolling up the sleeves of his rough blue jersey. Then he stooped, the muscles of his thighs tightening under his close-fitting trousers, to select a spar of wood as thick as his wrist and about two and a half feet long. He straightened up, hefting the bit of wood easily in his hand, and carefully keeping his eyes turned away from Christopher.

The man pulled reflectively on his beard and then, slowly, very slowly, took a pace towards Christopher. His foot seemed to rise for an hour and descend for a day, before he stood one pace nearer. Now the other foot rose with the unhurried deliberateness of a gas-balloon, and he was less than a yard from Christopher. As he started on his third pace, the hand that held the wooden stick began to rise towards his shoulder, and Christopher realized that he had reached the end of his quest.

So the hunt for the Great Auk had come to nothing, he thought, and then he remembered the story he had tried to recall before he set out. The story of the last Great Auk. The gaunt helpless bird, a captive in the fishermen's hut, while they, frightened by the storm, cursed it for a witch. The bird lying there for three days while the storm raged outside, and the men became more and more terrified. The leader in its capture now sneered at as the coward, recovering his dignity and seizing a piece of wood to belabour the bird for two hours until certain of its death.

The bearded man now stood straight above Christopher, and the stick was beginning, ever so slowly, to descend.

Christopher wished to meet his death bravely, but could not prevent the involuntary glance down at his body, a slight relief from the sight of the stick's inexorable descent.

He saw that the firm brown skin had receded from his wrists, and that short black feathers were growing there. Where one leg of his trousers had been pulled up, he saw, instead of the plump calf with short thin hairs, the wrinkled black of a bird's leg. He turned his eyes away, and, as he looked up to meet the falling bludgeon, felt his mouth being pulled out by some strange force into the semblance of a beak.

A CATALOGUE OF SELECTED DOVER BOOKS
IN ALL FIELDS OF INTEREST

A CATALOGUE OF SELECTED DOVER BOOKS
IN ALL FIELDS OF INTEREST

WHAT IS SCIENCE?, *N. Campbell*
The role of experiment and measurement, the function of mathematics, the nature of scientific laws, the difference between laws and theories, the limitations of science, and many similarly provocative topics are treated clearly and without technicalities by an eminent scientist. "Still an excellent introduction to scientific philosophy," H. Margenau in *Physics Today*. "A first-rate primer . . . deserves a wide audience," *Scientific American*. 192pp. 5⅜ x 8.
Paperbound $1.25

THE NATURE OF LIGHT AND COLOUR IN THE OPEN AIR, *M. Minnaert*
Why are shadows sometimes blue, sometimes green, or other colors depending on the light and surroundings? What causes mirages? Why do multiple suns and moons appear in the sky? Professor Minnaert explains these unusual phenomena and hundreds of others in simple, easy-to-understand terms based on optical laws and the properties of light and color. No mathematics is required but artists, scientists, students, and everyone fascinated by these "tricks" of nature will find thousands of useful and amazing pieces of information. Hundreds of observational experiments are suggested which require no special equipment. 200 illustrations; 42 photos. xvi + 362pp. 5⅜ x 8.
Paperbound $2.00

THE STRANGE STORY OF THE QUANTUM, AN ACCOUNT FOR THE GENERAL READER OF THE GROWTH OF IDEAS UNDERLYING OUR PRESENT ATOMIC KNOWLEDGE, *B. Hoffmann*
Presents lucidly and expertly, with barest amount of mathematics, the problems and theories which led to modern quantum physics. Dr. Hoffmann begins with the closing years of the 19th century, when certain trifling discrepancies were noticed, and with illuminating analogies and examples takes you through the brilliant concepts of Planck, Einstein, Pauli, Broglie, Bohr, Schroedinger, Heisenberg, Dirac, Sommerfeld, Feynman, etc. This edition includes a new, long postscript carrying the story through 1958. "Of the books attempting an account of the history and contents of our modern atomic physics which have come to my attention, this is the best," H. Margenau, Yale University, in *American Journal of Physics*. 32 tables and line illustrations. Index. 275pp. 5⅜ x 8.
Paperbound $1.75

GREAT IDEAS OF MODERN MATHEMATICS: THEIR NATURE AND USE, *Jagjit Singh*
Reader with only high school math will understand main mathematical ideas of modern physics, astronomy, genetics, psychology, evolution, etc. better than many who use them as tools, but comprehend little of their basic structure. Author uses his wide knowledge of non-mathematical fields in brilliant exposition of differential equations, matrices, group theory, logic, statistics, problems of mathematical foundations, imaginary numbers, vectors, etc. Original publication. 2 appendixes. 2 indexes. 65 ills. 322pp. 5⅜ x 8.
Paperbound $2.00

A SHORT ACCOUNT OF THE HISTORY OF MATHEMATICS,
W. W. Rouse Ball
Last previous edition (1908) hailed by mathematicians and laymen for lucid overview of math as living science, for understandable presentation of individual contributions of great mathematicians. Treats lives, discoveries of every important school and figure from Egypt, Phoenicia to late nineteenth century. Greek schools of Ionia, Cyzicus, Alexandria, Byzantium, Pythagoras; primitive arithmetic; Middle Ages and Renaissance, including European and Asiatic contributions; modern math of Descartes, Pascal, Wallis, Huygens, Newton, Euler, Lambert, Laplace, scores more. More emphasis on historical development, exposition of ideas than other books on subject. Non-technical, readable text can be followed with no more preparation than high-school algebra. Index. 544pp. 5⅜ x 8.   Paperbound $2.25

GREAT IDEAS AND THEORIES OF MODERN COSMOLOGY, *Jagjit Singh*
Companion volume to author's popular "Great Ideas of Modern Mathematics" (Dover, $2.00). The best non-technical survey of post-Einstein attempts to answer perhaps unanswerable questions of origin, age of Universe, possibility of life on other worlds, etc. Fundamental theories of cosmology and cosmogony recounted, explained, evaluated in light of most recent data: Einstein's concepts of relativity, space-time; Milne's a priori world-system; astrophysical theories of Jeans, Eddington; Hoyle's "continuous creation;" contributions of dozens more scientists. A faithful, comprehensive critical summary of complex material presented in an extremely well-written text intended for laymen. Original publication. Index. xii + 276pp. 5⅜ x 8½.   Paperbound $2.00

THE RESTLESS UNIVERSE, *Max Born*
A remarkably lucid account by a Nobel Laureate of recent theories of wave mechanics, behavior of gases, electrons and ions, waves and particles, electronic structure of the atom, nuclear physics, and similar topics. "Much more thorough and deeper than most attempts . . . easy and delightful," *Chemical and Engineering News*. Special feature: 7 animated sequences of 60 figures each showing such phenomena as gas molecules in motion, the scattering of alpha particles, etc. 11 full-page plates of photographs. Total of nearly 600 illustrations. 351pp. 6⅛ x 9¼.   Paperbound $2.00

PLANETS, STARS AND GALAXIES: DESCRIPTIVE ASTRONOMY FOR BEGINNERS,
A. E. Fanning
What causes the progression of the seasons? Phases of the moon? The Aurora Borealis? How much does the sun weigh? What are the chances of life on our sister planets? Absorbing introduction to astronomy, incorporating the latest discoveries and theories: the solar wind, the surface temperature of Venus, the pock-marked face of Mars, quasars, and much more. Places you on the frontiers of one of the most vital sciences of our time. Revised (1966). Introduction by Donald H. Menzel, Harvard University. References. Index. 45 illustrations. 189pp. 5¼ x 8¼.   Paperbound $1.50

GREAT IDEAS IN INFORMATION THEORY, LANGUAGE AND CYBERNETICS,
Jagjit Singh
Non-mathematical, but profound study of information, language, the codes used by men and machines to communicate, the principles of analog and digital computers, work of McCulloch, Pitts, von Neumann, Turing, and Uttley, correspondences between intricate mechanical network of "thinking machines" and more intricate neurophysiological mechanism of human brain. Indexes. 118 figures. 50 tables. ix + 338pp. 5⅜ x 8½.   Paperbound $2.00

THE MUSIC OF THE SPHERES: THE MATERIAL UNIVERSE — FROM ATOM TO QUASAR, SIMPLY EXPLAINED, *Guy Murchie*
Vast compendium of fact, modern concept and theory, observed and calculated data, historical background guides intelligent layman through the material universe. Brilliant exposition of earth's construction, explanations for moon's craters, atmospheric components of Venus and Mars (with data from recent fly-by's), sun spots, sequences of star birth and death, neighboring galaxies, contributions of Galileo, Tycho Brahe, Kepler, etc.; and (Vol. 2) construction of the atom (describing newly discovered sigma and xi subatomic particles), theories of sound, color and light, space and time, including relativity theory, quantum theory, wave theory, probability theory, work of Newton, Maxwell, Faraday, Einstein, de Broglie, etc. "Best presentation yet offered to the intelligent general reader," *Saturday Review*. Revised (1967). Index. 319 illustrations by the author. Total of xx + 644pp. 5⅜ x 8½.
Vol. 1 Paperbound $2.00, Vol. 2 Paperbound $2.00,
The set $4.00

FOUR LECTURES ON RELATIVITY AND SPACE, *Charles Proteus Steinmetz*
Lecture series, given by great mathematician and electrical engineer, generally considered one of the best popular-level expositions of special and general relativity theories and related questions. Steinmetz translates complex mathematical reasoning into language accessible to laymen through analogy, example and comparison. Among topics covered are relativity of motion, location, time; of mass; acceleration; 4-dimensional time-space; geometry of the gravitational field; curvature and bending of space; non-Euclidean geometry. Index. 40 illustrations. x + 142pp. 5⅜ x 8½.
Paperbound $1.35

HOW TO KNOW THE WILD FLOWERS, *Mrs. William Starr Dana*
Classic nature book that has introduced thousands to wonders of American wild flowers. Color-season principle of organization is easy to use, even by those with no botanical training, and the genial, refreshing discussions of history, folklore, uses of over 1,000 native and escape flowers, foliage plants are informative as well as fun to read. Over 170 full-page plates, collected from several editions, may be colored in to make permanent records of finds. Revised to conform with 1950 edition of Gray's Manual of Botany. xlii + 438pp. 5⅜ x 8½.
Paperbound $2.00

MANUAL OF THE TREES OF NORTH AMERICA, *Charles Sprague Sargent*
Still unsurpassed as most comprehensive, reliable study of North American tree characteristics, precise locations and distribution. By dean of American dendrologists. Every tree native to U.S., Canada, Alaska; 185 genera, 717 species, described in detail—leaves, flowers, fruit, winterbuds, bark, wood, growth habits, etc. plus discussion of varieties and local variants, immaturity variations. Over 100 keys, including unusual 11-page analytical key to genera, aid in identification. 783 clear illustrations of flowers, fruit, leaves. An unmatched permanent reference work for all nature lovers. Second enlarged (1926) edition. Synopsis of families. Analytical key to genera. Glossary of technical terms. Index. 783 illustrations, 1 map. Total of 982pp. 5⅜ x 8.
Vol. 1 Paperbound $2.25, Vol. 2 Paperbound $2.25,
The set $4.50

IT'S FUN TO MAKE THINGS FROM SCRAP MATERIALS,
Evelyn Glantz Hershoff
What use are empty spools, tin cans, bottle tops? What can be made from rubber bands, clothes pins, paper clips, and buttons? This book provides simply worded instructions and large diagrams showing you how to make cookie cutters, toy trucks, paper turkeys, Halloween masks, telephone sets, aprons, linoleum block- and spatter prints — in all 399 projects! Many are easy enough for young children to figure out for themselves; some challenging enough to entertain adults; all are remarkably ingenious ways to make things from materials that cost pennies or less! Formerly "Scrap Fun for Everyone." Index. 214 illustrations. 373pp. 5⅜ x 8½.   Paperbound $1.50

SYMBOLIC LOGIC and THE GAME OF LOGIC, *Lewis Carroll*
"Symbolic Logic" is not concerned with modern symbolic logic, but is instead a collection of over 380 problems posed with charm and imagination, using the syllogism and a fascinating diagrammatic method of drawing conclusions. In "The Game of Logic" Carroll's whimsical imagination devises a logical game played with 2 diagrams and counters (included) to manipulate hundreds of tricky syllogisms. The final section, "Hit or Miss" is a lagniappe of 101 additional puzzles in the delightful Carroll manner. Until this reprint edition, both of these books were rarities costing up to $15 each. Symbolic Logic: Index. xxxi + 199pp. The Game of Logic: 96pp. 2 vols. bound as one. 5⅜ x 8.
Paperbound $2.00

MATHEMATICAL PUZZLES OF SAM LOYD, PART I
selected and edited by M. Gardner
Choice puzzles by the greatest American puzzle creator and innovator. Selected from his famous collection, "Cyclopedia of Puzzles," they retain the unique style and historical flavor of the originals. There are posers based on arithmetic, algebra, probability, game theory, route tracing, topology, counter and sliding block, operations research, geometrical dissection. Includes the famous "14-15" puzzle which was a national craze, and his "Horse of a Different Color" which sold millions of copies. 117 of his most ingenious puzzles in all. 120 line drawings and diagrams. Solutions. Selected references. xx + 167pp. 5⅜ x 8.
Paperbound $1.00

STRING FIGURES AND HOW TO MAKE THEM, *Caroline Furness Jayne*
107 string figures plus variations selected from the best primitive and modern examples developed by Navajo, Apache, pygmies of Africa, Eskimo, in Europe, Australia, China, etc. The most readily understandable, easy-to-follow book in English on perennially popular recreation. Crystal-clear exposition; step-by-step diagrams. Everyone from kindergarten children to adults looking for unusual diversion will be endlessly amused. Index. Bibliography. Introduction by A. C. Haddon. 17 full-page plates, 960 illustrations. xxiii + 401pp. 5⅜ x 8½.
Paperbound $2.00

PAPER FOLDING FOR BEGINNERS, *W. D. Murray and F. J. Rigney*
A delightful introduction to the varied and entertaining Japanese art of origami (paper folding), with a full, crystal-clear text that anticipates every difficulty; over 275 clearly labeled diagrams of all important stages in creation. You get results at each stage, since complex figures are logically developed from simpler ones. 43 different pieces are explained: sailboats, frogs, roosters, etc. 6 photographic plates. 279 diagrams. 95pp. 5⅝ x 8⅜. Paperbound $1.00

PRINCIPLES OF ART HISTORY,
H. Wölfflin
Analyzing such terms as "baroque," "classic," "neoclassic," "primitive," "picturesque," and 164 different works by artists like Botticelli, van Cleve, Dürer, Hobbema, Holbein, Hals, Rembrandt, Titian, Brueghel, Vermeer, and many others, the author establishes the classifications of art history and style on a firm, concrete basis. This classic of art criticism shows what really occurred between the 14th-century primitives and the sophistication of the 18th century in terms of basic attitudes and philosophies. "A remarkable lesson in the art of seeing," *Sat. Rev. of Literature.* Translated from the 7th German edition. 150 illustrations. 254pp. 6⅛ x 9¼. Paperbound $2.00

PRIMITIVE ART,
Franz Boas
This authoritative and exhaustive work by a great American anthropologist covers the entire gamut of primitive art. Pottery, leatherwork, metal work, stone work, wood, basketry, are treated in detail. Theories of primitive art, historical depth in art history, technical virtuosity, unconscious levels of patterning, symbolism, styles, literature, music, dance, etc. A must book for the interested layman, the anthropologist, artist, handicrafter (hundreds of unusual motifs), and the historian. Over 900 illustrations (50 ceramic vessels, 12 totem poles, etc.) 376pp. 5⅜ x 8. Paperbound $2.25

THE GENTLEMAN AND CABINET MAKER'S DIRECTOR,
Thomas Chippendale
A reprint of the 1762 catalogue of furniture designs that went on to influence generations of English and Colonial and Early Republic American furniture makers. The 200 plates, most of them full-page sized, show Chippendale's designs for French (Louis XV), Gothic, and Chinese-manner chairs, sofas, canopy and dome beds, cornices, chamber organs, cabinets, shaving tables, commodes, picture frames, frets, candle stands, chimney pieces, decorations, etc. The drawings are all elegant and highly detailed; many include construction diagrams and elevations. A supplement of 24 photographs shows surviving pieces of original and Chippendale-style pieces of furniture. Brief biography of Chippendale by N. I. Bienenstock, editor of *Furniture World.* Reproduced from the 1762 edition. 200 plates, plus 19 photographic plates. vi + 249pp. 9⅛ x 12¼. Paperbound $3.50

AMERICAN ANTIQUE FURNITURE: A BOOK FOR AMATEURS,
Edgar G. Miller, Jr.
Standard introduction and practical guide to identification of valuable American antique furniture. 2115 illustrations, mostly photographs taken by the author in 148 private homes, are arranged in chronological order in extensive chapters on chairs, sofas, chests, desks, bedsteads, mirrors, tables, clocks, and other articles. Focus is on furniture accessible to the collector, including simpler pieces and a larger than usual coverage of Empire style. Introductory chapters identify structural elements, characteristics of various styles, how to avoid fakes, etc. "We are frequently asked to name some book on American furniture that will meet the requirements of the novice collector, the beginning dealer, and . . . the general public. . . . We believe Mr. Miller's two volumes more completely satisfy this specification than any other work," *Antiques.* Appendix. Index. Total of vi + 1106pp. 7⅞ x 10¾.
Two volume set, paperbound $7.50

THE BAD CHILD'S BOOK OF BEASTS, MORE BEASTS FOR WORSE CHILDREN, and A MORAL ALPHABET, *H. Belloc*

Hardly and anthology of humorous verse has appeared in the last 50 years without at least a couple of these famous nonsense verses. But one must see the entire volumes — with all the delightful original illustrations by Sir Basil Blackwood — to appreciate fully Belloc's charming and witty verses that play so subacidly on the platitudes of life and morals that beset his day — and ours. A great humor classic. Three books in one. Total of 157pp. 5⅜ x 8.

Paperbound $1.00

THE DEVIL'S DICTIONARY, *Ambrose Bierce*

Sardonic and irreverent barbs puncturing the pomposities and absurdities of American politics, business, religion, literature, and arts, by the country's greatest satirist in the classic tradition. Epigrammatic as Shaw, piercing as Swift, American as Mark Twain, Will Rogers, and Fred Allen, Bierce will always remain the favorite of a small coterie of enthusiasts, and of writers and speakers whom he supplies with "some of the most gorgeous witticisms of the English language" (H. L. Mencken). Over 1000 entries in alphabetical order. 144pp. 5⅜ x 8.

Paperbound $1.00

THE COMPLETE NONSENSE OF EDWARD LEAR.

This is the only complete edition of this master of gentle madness available at a popular price. *A Book of Nonsense, Nonsense Songs, More Nonsense Songs and Stories* in their entirety with all the old favorites that have delighted children and adults for years. The Dong With A Luminous Nose, The Jumblies, The Owl and the Pussycat, and hundreds of other bits of wonderful nonsense. 214 limericks, 3 sets of Nonsense Botany, 5 Nonsense Alphabets, 546 drawings by Lear himself, and much more. 320pp. 5⅜ x 8.

Paperbound $1.00

THE WIT AND HUMOR OF OSCAR WILDE, *ed. by Alvin Redman*

Wilde at his most brilliant, in 1000 epigrams exposing weaknesses and hypocrisies of "civilized" society. Divided into 49 categories—sin, wealth, women, America, etc.—to aid writers, speakers. Includes excerpts from his trials, books, plays, criticism. Formerly "The Epigrams of Oscar Wilde." Introduction by Vyvyan Holland, Wilde's only living son. Introductory essay by editor. 260pp. 5⅜ x 8.

Paperbound $1.00

A CHILD'S PRIMER OF NATURAL HISTORY, *Oliver Herford*

Scarcely an anthology of whimsy and humor has appeared in the last 50 years without a contribution from Oliver Herford. Yet the works from which these examples are drawn have been almost impossible to obtain! Here at last are Herford's improbable definitions of a menagerie of familiar and weird animals, each verse illustrated by the author's own drawings. 24 drawings in 2 colors; 24 additional drawings. vii + 95pp. 6½ x 6.

Paperbound $1.00

THE BROWNIES: THEIR BOOK, *Palmer Cox*

The book that made the Brownies a household word. Generations of readers have enjoyed the antics, predicaments and adventures of these jovial sprites, who emerge from the forest at night to play or to come to the aid of a deserving human. Delightful illustrations by the author decorate nearly every page. 24 short verse tales with 266 illustrations. 155pp. 6⅝ x 9¼.

Paperbound $1.50

THE PRINCIPLES OF PSYCHOLOGY,
William James
The full long-course, unabridged, of one of the great classics of Western literature and science. Wonderfully lucid descriptions of human mental activity, the stream of thought, consciousness, time perception, memory, imagination, emotions, reason, abnormal phenomena, and similar topics. Original contributions are integrated with the work of such men as Berkeley, Binet, Mills, Darwin, Hume, Kant, Royce, Schopenhauer, Spinoza, Locke, Descartes, Galton, Wundt, Lotze, Herbart, Fechner, and scores of others. All contrasting interpretations of mental phenomena are examined in detail—introspective analysis, philosophical interpretation, and experimental research. "A classic," *Journal of Consulting Psychology.* "The main lines are as valid as ever," *Psychoanalytical Quarterly.* "Standard reading . . . a classic of interpretation," *Psychiatric Quarterly.* 94 illustrations. 1408pp. 5⅜ x 8.
Vol. 1 Paperbound $2.50, Vol. 2 Paperbound $2.50,
The set $5.00

VISUAL ILLUSIONS: THEIR CAUSES, CHARACTERISTICS AND APPLICATIONS,
M. Luckiesh
"Seeing is deceiving," asserts the author of this introduction to virtually every type of optical illusion known. The text both describes and explains the principles involved in color illusions, figure-ground, distance illusions, etc. 100 photographs, drawings and diagrams prove how easy it is to fool the sense: circles that aren't round, parallel lines that seem to bend, stationary figures that seem to move as you stare at them — illustration after illustration strains our credulity at what we see. Fascinating book from many points of view, from applications for artists, in camouflage, etc. to the psychology of vision. New introduction by William Ittleson, Dept. of Psychology, Queens College. Index. Bibliography. xxi + 252pp. 5⅜ x 8½.   Paperbound $1.50

FADS AND FALLACIES IN THE NAME OF SCIENCE,
Martin Gardner
This is the standard account of various cults, quack systems, and delusions which have masqueraded as science: hollow earth fanatics. Reich and orgone sex energy, dianetics, Atlantis, multiple moons, Forteanism, flying saucers, medical fallacies like iridiagnosis, zone therapy, etc. A new chapter has been added on Bridey Murphy, psionics, and other recent manifestations in this field. This is a fair, reasoned appraisal of eccentric theory which provides excellent inoculation against cleverly masked nonsense. "Should be read by everyone, scientist and non-scientist alike," R. T. Birge, Prof. Emeritus of Physics, Univ. of California; Former President, American Physical Society. Index. x + 365pp. 5⅜ x 8.   Paperbound $1.85

ILLUSIONS AND DELUSIONS OF THE SUPERNATURAL AND THE OCCULT,
D. H. Rawcliffe
Holds up to rational examination hundreds of persistent delusions including crystal gazing, automatic writing, table turning, mediumistic trances, mental healing, stigmata, lycanthropy, live burial, the Indian Rope Trick, spiritualism, dowsing, telepathy, clairvoyance, ghosts, ESP, etc. The author explains and exposes the mental and physical deceptions involved, making this not only an exposé of supernatural phenomena, but a valuable exposition of characteristic types of abnormal psychology. Originally titled "The Psychology of the Occult." 14 illustrations. Index. 551pp. 5⅜ x 8.   Paperbound $2.25

FAIRY TALE COLLECTIONS, *edited by Andrew Lang*
Andrew Lang's fairy tale collections make up the richest shelf-full of traditional children's stories anywhere available. Lang supervised the translation of stories from all over the world—familiar European tales collected by Grimm, animal stories from Negro Africa, myths of primitive Australia, stories from Russia, Hungary, Iceland, Japan, and many other countries. Lang's selection of translations are unusually high; many authorities consider that the most familiar tales find their best versions in these volumes. All collections are richly decorated and illustrated by H. J. Ford and other artists.

THE BLUE FAIRY BOOK. 37 stories. 138 illustrations. ix + 390pp. 5⅜ x 8½.
Paperbound $1.50

THE GREEN FAIRY BOOK. 42 stories. 100 illustrations. xiii + 366pp. 5⅜ x 8½.
Paperbound $1.50

THE BROWN FAIRY BOOK. 32 stories. 50 illustrations, 8 in color. xii + 350pp. 5⅜ x 8½.
Paperbound $1.50

THE BEST TALES OF HOFFMANN, *edited by E. F. Bleiler*
10 stories by E. T. A. Hoffmann, one of the greatest of all writers of fantasy. The tales include "The Golden Flower Pot," "Automata," "A New Year's Eve Adventure," "Nutcracker and the King of Mice," "Sand-Man," and others. Vigorous characterizations of highly eccentric personalities, remarkably imaginative situations, and intensely fast pacing has made these tales popular all over the world for 150 years. Editor's introduction. 7 drawings by Hoffmann. xxxiii + 419pp. 5⅜ x 8½.
Paperbound $2.00

GHOST AND HORROR STORIES OF AMBROSE BIERCE,
edited by E. F. Bleiler
Morbid, eerie, horrifying tales of possessed poets, shabby aristocrats, revived corpses, and haunted malefactors. Widely acknowledged as the best of their kind between Poe and the moderns, reflecting their author's inner torment and bitter view of life. Includes "Damned Thing," "The Middle Toe of the Right Foot," "The Eyes of the Panther," "Visions of the Night," "Moxon's Master," and over a dozen others. Editor's introduction. xxii + 199pp. 5⅜ x 8½.
Paperbound $1.25

THREE GOTHIC NOVELS, *edited by E. F. Bleiler*
Originators of the still popular Gothic novel form, influential in ushering in early 19th-century Romanticism. Horace Walpole's *Castle of Otranto*, William Beckford's *Vathek*, John Polidori's *The Vampyre*, and a *Fragment* by Lord Byron are enjoyable as exciting reading or as documents in the history of English literature. Editor's introduction. xi + 291pp. 5⅜ x 8½.
Paperbound $2.00

BEST GHOST STORIES OF LEFANU, *edited by E. F. Bleiler*
Though admired by such critics as V. S. Pritchett, Charles Dickens and Henry James, ghost stories by the Irish novelist Joseph Sheridan LeFanu have never become as widely known as his detective fiction. About half of the 16 stories in this collection have never before been available in America. Collection includes "Carmilla" (perhaps the best vampire story ever written), "The Haunted Baronet," "The Fortunes of Sir Robert Ardagh," and the classic "Green Tea." Editor's introduction. 7 contemporary illustrations. Portrait of LeFanu. xii + 467pp. 5⅜ x 8.
Paperbound $2.00

EASY-TO-DO ENTERTAINMENTS AND DIVERSIONS WITH COINS, CARDS, STRING, PAPER AND MATCHES, *R. M. Abraham*
Over 300 tricks, games and puzzles will provide young readers with absorbing fun. Sections on card games; paper-folding; tricks with coins, matches and pieces of string; games for the agile; toy-making from common household objects; mathematical recreations; and 50 miscellaneous pastimes. Anyone in charge of groups of youngsters, including hard-pressed parents, and in need of suggestions on how to keep children sensibly amused and quietly content will find this book indispensable. Clear, simple text, copious number of delightful line drawings and illustrative diagrams. Originally titled "Winter Nights' Entertainments." Introduction by Lord Baden Powell. 329 illustrations. v + 186pp. 5⅜ x 8½. Paperbound $1.00

AN INTRODUCTION TO CHESS MOVES AND TACTICS SIMPLY EXPLAINED, *Leonard Barden*
Beginner's introduction to the royal game. Names, possible moves of the pieces, definitions of essential terms, how games are won, etc. explained in 30-odd pages. With this background you'll be able to sit right down and play. Balance of book teaches strategy — openings, middle game, typical endgame play, and suggestions for improving your game. A sample game is fully analyzed. True middle-level introduction, teaching you all the essentials without oversimplifying or losing you in a maze of detail. 58 figures. 102pp. 5⅜ x 8½. Paperbound $1.00

LASKER'S MANUAL OF CHESS, *Dr. Emanuel Lasker*
Probably the greatest chess player of modern times, Dr. Emanuel Lasker held the world championship 28 years, independent of passing schools or fashions. This unmatched study of the game, chiefly for intermediate to skilled players, analyzes basic methods, combinations, position play, the aesthetics of chess, dozens of different openings, etc., with constant reference to great modern games. Contains a brilliant exposition of Steinitz's important theories. Introduction by Fred Reinfeld. Tables of Lasker's tournament record. 3 indices. 308 diagrams. 1 photograph. xxx + 349pp. 5⅜ x 8. Paperbound $2.25

COMBINATIONS: THE HEART OF CHESS, *Irving Chernev*
Step-by-step from simple combinations to complex, this book, by a well-known chess writer, shows you the intricacies of pins, counter-pins, knight forks, and smothered mates. Other chapters show alternate lines of play to those taken in actual championship games; boomerang combinations; classic examples of brilliant combination play by Nimzovich, Rubinstein, Tarrasch, Botvinnik, Alekhine and Capablanca. Index. 356 diagrams. ix + 245pp. 5⅜ x 8½. Paperbound $1.85

HOW TO SOLVE CHESS PROBLEMS, *K. S. Howard*
Full of practical suggestions for the fan or the beginner — who knows only the moves of the chessmen. Contains preliminary section and 58 two-move, 46 three-move, and 8 four-move problems composed by 27 outstanding American problem creators in the last 30 years. Explanation of all terms and exhaustive index. "Just what is wanted for the student," Brian Harley. 112 problems, solutions. vi + 171pp. 5⅜ x 8. Paperbound $1.35

SOCIAL THOUGHT FROM LORE TO SCIENCE,
H. E. Barnes and H. Becker
An immense survey of sociological thought and ways of viewing, studying, planning, and reforming society from earliest times to the present. Includes thought on society of preliterate peoples, ancient non-Western cultures, and every great movement in Europe, America, and modern Japan. Analyzes hundreds of great thinkers: Plato, Augustine, Bodin, Vico, Montesquieu, Herder, Comte, Marx, etc. Weighs the contributions of utopians, sophists, fascists and communists; economists, jurists, philosophers, ecclesiastics, and every 19th and 20th century school of scientific sociology, anthropology, and social psychology throughout the world. Combines topical, chronological, and regional approaches, treating the evolution of social thought as a process rather than as a series of mere topics. "Impressive accuracy, competence, and discrimination . . . easily the best single survey," Nation. Thoroughly revised, with new material up to 1960. 2 indexes. Over 2200 bibliographical notes. Three volume set. Total of 1586pp. 5⅜ x 8.
Vol. 1 Paperbound $2.75, Vol. 2 Paperbound $2.75, Vol. 3 Paperbound $2.50
The set $8.00

A HISTORY OF HISTORICAL WRITING, Harry Elmer Barnes
Virtually the only adequate survey of the whole course of historical writing in a single volume. Surveys developments from the beginnings of historiography in the ancient Near East and the Classical World, up through the Cold War. Covers major historians in detail, shows interrelationship with cultural background, makes clear individual contributions, evaluates and estimates importance; also enormously rich upon minor authors and thinkers who are usually passed over. Packed with scholarship and learning, clear, easily written. Indispensable to every student of history. Revised and enlarged up to 1961. Index and bibliography. xv + 442pp. 5⅜ x 8½.   Paperbound $2.50

JOHANN SEBASTIAN BACH, Philipp Spitta
The complete and unabridged text of the definitive study of Bach. Written some 70 years ago, it is still unsurpassed for its coverage of nearly all aspects of Bach's life and work. There could hardly be a finer non-technical introduction to Bach's music than the detailed, lucid analyses which Spitta provides for hundreds of individual pieces. 26 solid pages are devoted to the B minor mass, for example, and 30 pages to the glorious St. Matthew Passion. This monumental set also includes a major analysis of the music of the 18th century: Buxtehude, Pachelbel, etc. "Unchallenged as the last word on one of the supreme geniuses of music," John Barkham, Saturday Review Syndicate. Total of 1819pp. Heavy cloth binding. 5⅜ x 8.
Two volume set, clothbound $13.50

BEETHOVEN AND HIS NINE SYMPHONIES, George Grove
In this modern middle-level classic of musicology Grove not only analyzes all nine of Beethoven's symphonies very thoroughly in terms of their musical structure, but also discusses the circumstances under which they were written, Beethoven's stylistic development, and much other background material. This is an extremely rich book, yet very easily followed; it is highly recommended to anyone seriously interested in music. Over 250 musical passages. Index. viii + 407pp. 5⅜ x 8.   Paperbound $2.00

THREE SCIENCE FICTION NOVELS,
John Taine
Acknowledged by many as the best SF writer of the 1920's, Taine (under the name Eric Temple Bell) was also a Professor of Mathematics of considerable renown. Reprinted here are *The Time Stream*, generally considered Taine's best, *The Greatest Game*, a biological-fiction novel, and *The Purple Sapphire*, involving a supercivilization of the past. Taine's stories tie fantastic narratives to frameworks of original and logical scientific concepts. Speculation is often profound on such questions as the nature of time, concept of entropy, cyclical universes, etc. 4 contemporary illustrations. v + 532pp. 5⅜ x 8⅜.
T1180   Paperbound $2.00

SEVEN SCIENCE FICTION NOVELS,
H. G. Wells
Full unabridged texts of 7 science-fiction novels of the master. Ranging from biology, physics, chemistry, astronomy, to sociology and other studies, Mr. Wells extrapolates whole worlds of strange and intriguing character. "One will have to go far to match this for entertainment, excitement, and sheer pleasure . . ."*New York Times.* Contents: The Time Machine, The Island of Dr. Moreau, The First Men in the Moon, The Invisible Man, The War of the Worlds, The Food of the Gods, In The Days of the Comet. 1015pp. 5⅜ x 8.
T264   Clothbound $5.00

28 SCIENCE FICTION STORIES OF H. G. WELLS.
Two full, unabridged novels, *Men Like Gods* and *Star Begotten,* plus 26 short stories by the master science-fiction writer of all time! Stories of space, time, invention, exploration, futuristic adventure. Partial contents: *The Country of the Blind, In the Abyss, The Crystal Egg, The Man Who Could Work Miracles, A Story of Days to Come, The Empire of the Ants, The Magic Shop, The Valley of the Spiders, A Story of the Stone Age, Under the Knife, Sea Raiders,* etc. An indispensable collection for the library of anyone interested in science fiction adventure. 928pp. 5⅜ x 8.   T265   Clothbound $5.00

THREE MARTIAN NOVELS,
Edgar Rice Burroughs
Complete, unabridged reprinting, in one volume, of Thuvia, Maid of Mars; Chessmen of Mars; The Master Mind of Mars. Hours of science-fiction adventure by a modern master storyteller. Reset in large clear type for easy reading. 16 illustrations by J. Allen St. John. vi + 490pp. 5⅜ x 8½.
T39   Paperbound $2.50

AN INTELLECTUAL AND CULTURAL HISTORY OF THE WESTERN WORLD,
Harry Elmer Barnes
Monumental 3-volume survey of intellectual development of Europe from primitive cultures to the present day. Every significant product of human intellect traced through history: art, literature, mathematics, physical sciences, medicine, music, technology, social sciences, religions, jurisprudence, education, etc. Presentation is lucid and specific, analyzing in detail specific discoveries, theories, literary works, and so on. Revised (1965) by recognized scholars in specialized fields under the direction of Prof. Barnes. Revised bibliography. Indexes. 24 illustrations. Total of xxix + 1318pp.
T1275, T1276, T1277   Three volume set, paperbound $7.50

HEAR ME TALKIN' TO YA, *edited by Nat Shapiro and Nat Hentoff*
In their own words, Louis Armstrong, King Oliver, Fletcher Henderson, Bunk
Johnson, Bix Beiderbecke, Billy Holiday, Fats Waller, Jelly Roll Morton,
Duke Ellington, and many others comment on the origins of jazz in New
Orleans and its growth in Chicago's South Side, Kansas City's jam sessions,
Depression Harlem, and the modernism of the West Coast schools. Taken
from taped conversations, letters, magazine articles, other first-hand sources.
Editors' introduction. xvi + 429pp. 5⅜ x 8½.   T1726   Paperbound $2.00

THE JOURNAL OF HENRY D. THOREAU
A 25-year record by the great American observer and critic, as complete a
record of a great man's inner life as is anywhere available. Thoreau's Journals
served him as raw material for his formal pieces, as a place where he could
develop his ideas, as an outlet for his interests in wild life and plants, in
writing as an art, in classics of literature, Walt Whitman and other contemporaries, in politics, slavery, individual's relation to the State, etc. The
Journals present a portrait of a remarkable man, and are an observant social
history. Unabridged republication of 1906 edition, Bradford Torrey and
Francis H. Allen, editors. Illustrations. Total of 1888pp. 8⅜ x 12¼.
                            T312, T313   Two volume set, clothbound $25.00

A SHAKESPEARIAN GRAMMAR, *E. A. Abbott*
Basic reference to Shakespeare and his contemporaries, explaining through
thousands of quotations from Shakespeare, Jonson, Beaumont and Fletcher,
North's *Plutarch* and other sources the grammatical usage differing from the
modern. First published in 1870 and written by a scholar who spent much of
his life isolating principles of Elizabethan language, the book is unlikely ever
to be superseded. Indexes. xxiv + 511pp. 5⅜ x 8½. T1582 Paperbound $2.75

FOLK-LORE OF SHAKESPEARE, *T. F. Thistelton Dyer*
Classic study, drawing from Shakespeare a large body of references to supernatural beliefs, terminology of falconry and hunting, games and sports, good
luck charms, marriage customs, folk medicines, superstitions about plants,
animals, birds, argot of the underworld, sexual slang of London, proverbs,
drinking customs, weather lore, and much else. From full compilation comes
a mirror of the 17th-century popular mind. Index. ix + 526pp. 5⅜ x 8½.
                            T1614   Paperbound $2.75

THE NEW VARIORUM SHAKESPEARE, *edited by H. H. Furness*
By far the richest editions of the plays ever produced in any country or
language. Each volume contains complete text (usually First Folio) of the
play, all variants in Quarto and other Folio texts, editorial changes by every
major editor to Furness's own time (1900), footnotes to obscure references or
language, extensive quotes from literature of Shakespearian criticism, essays
on plot sources (often reprinting sources in full), and much more.

HAMLET, *edited by H. H. Furness*
Total of xxvi + 905pp. 5⅜ x 8½.
                    T1004, T1005   Two volume set, paperbound $5.25

TWELFTH NIGHT, *edited by H. H. Furness*
Index. xxii + 434pp. 5⅜ x 8½.   T1189   Paperbound $2.75

CATALOGUE OF DOVER BOOKS

LA BOHEME BY GIACOMO PUCCINI,
translated and introduced by Ellen H. Bleiler
Complete handbook for the operagoer, with everything needed for full enjoy-
ment except the musical score itself. Complete Italian libretto, with new,
modern English line-by-line translation—the only libretto printing all repeats;
biography of Puccini; the librettists; background to the opera, Murger's La
Boheme, etc.; circumstances of composition and performances; plot summary;
and pictorial section of 73 illustrations showing Puccini, famous singers and
performances, etc. Large clear type for easy reading. 124pp. 5⅜ x 8½.
                                                    T404   Paperbound $1.00

ANTONIO STRADIVARI: HIS LIFE AND WORK (1644-1737),
W. Henry Hill, Arthur F. Hill, and Alfred E. Hill
Still the only book that really delves into life and art of the incomparable
Italian craftsman, maker of the finest musical instruments in the world today.
The authors, expert violin-makers themselves, discuss Stradivari's ancestry, his
construction and finishing techniques, distinguished characteristics of many
of his instruments and their locations. Included, too, is story of introduction
of his. instruments into France, England, first revelation of their supreme
merit, and information on his labels, number of instruments made, prices,
mystery of ingredients of his varnish, tone of pre-1684 Stradivari violin and
changes between 1684 and 1690. An extremely interesting, informative account
for all music lovers, from craftsman to concert-goer. Republication of original
(1902) edition. New introduction by Sydney Beck, Head of Rare Book and
Manuscript Collections, Music Division, New York Public Library. Analytical
index by Rembert Wurlitzer. Appendixes. 68 illustrations. 30 full-page plates.
4 in color. xxvi + 315pp. 5⅜ x 8½.   T425   Paperbound $2.25

MUSICAL AUTOGRAPHS FROM MONTEVERDI TO HINDEMITH,
Emanuel Winternitz
For beauty, for intrinsic interest, for perspective on the composer's personality,
for subtleties of phrasing, shading, emphasis indicated in the autograph but
suppressed in the printed score, the mss. of musical composition are fascinating
documents which repay close study in many different ways. This 2-volume
work reprints facsimiles of mss. by virtually every major composer, and many
minor figures—196 examples in all. A full text points out what can be learned
from mss., analyzes each sample. Index. Bibliography. 18 figures. 196 plates.
Total of 170pp. of text. 7⅞ x 10¾.
                               T1312, T1313   Two volume set, paperbound $4.00

J. S. BACH,
Albert Schweitzer
One of the few great full-length studies of Bach's life and work, and the
study upon which Schweitzer's renown as a musicologist rests. On first appearance (1911), revolutionized Bach performance. The only writer on Bach to
be musicologist, performing musician, and student of history, theology and
philosophy, Schweitzer contributes particularly full sections on history of German Protestant church music, theories on motivic pictorial representations
in vocal music, and practical suggestions for performance. Translated by
Ernest Newman. Indexes. 5 illustrations. 650 musical examples. Total of xix
+ 928pp. 5⅜ x 8½.   T1631, T1632   Two volume set, paperbound $4.50

TREES OF THE EASTERN AND CENTRAL UNITED STATES AND CANADA, *W. M. Harlow*
A revised edition of a standard middle-level guide to native trees and important escapes. More than 140 trees are described in detail, and illustrated with more than 600 drawings and photographs. Supplementary keys will enable the careful reader to identify almost any tree he might encounter. xiii + 288pp. 5⅜ x 8.   Paperbound $1.45

INSECT LIFE AND INSECT NATURAL HISTORY, *S. W. Frost*
A work emphasizing habits, social life, and ecological relations of insects, rather than more academic aspects of classification and morphology. Prof. Frost's enthusiasm and knowledge are everywhere evident as he discusses insect associations and specialized habits like leaf-rolling, leaf-mining, and case-making, the gall insects, the boring insects, aquatic insects, etc. He examines all sorts of matters not usually covered in general works such as: insects as human food, insect music and musicians, insect response to electric and radio waves, use of insects in art and literature. The admirably executed purpose of this book, which covers the middle ground between elementary treatment and scholarly monographs, is to excite the reader to observe for himself. Over 700 illustrations. Extensive bibliography. x + 542pp. 5⅜ x 8.   Paperbound $2.50

HANDBOOK OF BIRDS OF EASTERN NORTH AMERICA, *Frank M. Chapman*
Formerly *the* field guide to Eastern birds. Still contains most complete descriptions of plumages, behavior, nest and eggs, habitat, etc. as observed in the field by Chapman and other important ornithologists. Generally, the most comprehensive compendium of bird lore available in the handbook format. Color keys. Illustrated synopsis of orders and suborders. Index. 195 illustrations. xxxvi + 581pp. 5⅜ x 8½.   Paperbound $3.25

LIFE HISTORIES OF NORTH AMERICAN BIRDS, *Arthur Cleveland Bent*
Monumental series of books on North American birds, prepared and published under auspices of Smithsonian Institution. The definitive coverage of the subject; the most-used single source of information. Entire 22-volume set now available from Dover in inexpensive paperbound format. An encyclopedic collection of detailed, specific observations utilizing reports of hundreds of contemporary observers, writings of such naturalists as Audubon, Burroughs, William Brewster, as well as author's own extensive investigations. Contains literally everything known about life history of each bird considered (over 1160 species): nesting, eggs, plumage, distribution and migration, voice, enemies, courtship display, etc. Each volume fully illustrated with up to 393 photographs.   22-volume complete set, Paperbound $59.95

Prices subject to change without notice.

Available at your book dealer or write for free catalogue to Dept. Adsci, Dover Publications, Inc., 180 Varick St., N.Y., N.Y. 10014. Dover publishes more than 150 books each year on science, elementary and advanced mathematics, biology, music, art, literary history, social sciences and other areas.